WORK GOOD

Andy Bracken

A Morning Brake Book

ISBN: 9781098872588

First Edition.

For C & R. With love.
x

Thanks to Cathy for the cover image. I always told her she could draw like a five-year-old.

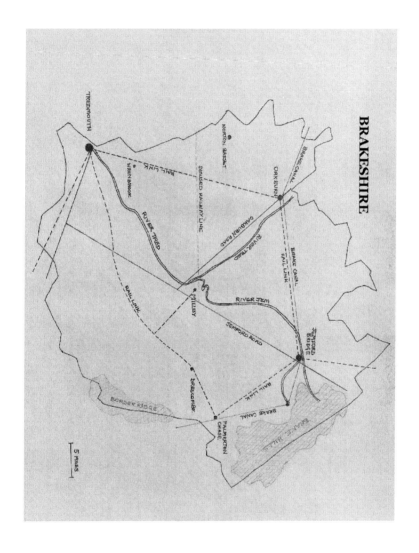

1.

There's nothing worth getting up for.

It's a Sunday. A non-work day. So I lie in bed.

Work, apparently, is worth getting up for.

It isn't. It's shit, and I detest it. But it earns the money that I need to survive.

Survival. That's the name of the game. It's what life's all about. My sole purpose every day, is to simply keep fucking going.

My old man, and his before him, actually enjoyed their work. They belonged to a different generation, I suppose.

They remembered wars, both World and Cold, whereby their very existence was in peril every minute of every day. One rogue Luftwaffe bomb, or some power-crazed Stalinist with his finger on a button, and it was all over for them. Boom!

So, yeah, just being able to get up and go to work was a blessing. Do your bit. Help to rebuild the nation. Play your part. Pay your taxes. Fund the NHS and the welfare system.

They earned the freedoms that I enjoy.

And, because I'm free, I can enjoy a lie in bed for as long as I like on a non-work day.

This is my day. A day of rest.

I worked for five days. Plus a half day unpaid on Saturday. Catching up. Dad would be proud.

If he wasn't dead, he'd be proud.

All that work put him in an early grave.

Bills to pay. A roof over our heads. Food in our bellies. School uniforms and shoes to be bought. The cycle of life, as I got the education he never did. All so I might be better.

Betterment - that was his objective, as far as I can understand it.

He was a mechanic. Nothing fancy. Just cars. Oil and grease were his ink and cappuccino. The sprinkles were fragments off the welder that left debris behind his left eye.

Vivid is the memory of the smell of his hands.

Apart from on a Sunday. Like me, it was his day of rest.

On a Saturday afternoon, he'd come home from work and soak in a bath for an hour, topping the water up every ten minutes. Gurgle, gurgle. He'd steep the crap out of his skin and hair.

A different man would emerge. He could never rid himself of all the stains, but he'd scrub himself hard enough so that pink would predominate his complexion.

All that effort for one day off. Come the Monday, the overalls would be back on, and the aromas would taint him once again.

The difference is, on his day off, he didn't lie in bed all morning.

The green glow of the clock in my shrouded chamber informs me that it's ten past ten. A throbbing colon declares the passing of every second. The morning isn't over yet. There's still time.

Still time for what?

I could lie here for another twenty minutes, and hatch all manner of schemes. It's easy, lying here and making plans. But the best laid plans, and all that.

This is the best time. Here and now, everything is possible. As soon as I get up, life will get in the way.

On rising, I'll lose the will. A jadedness will descend. A self-defeatism will bubble to the fore, and I'll know that it isn't worth starting anything.

After all, why begin something I shall never finish?

Anything I can think needs doing are big things. They shan't be completed in a day. And a day is all I have. Come tomorrow, the shit-storm starts again.

I deserve a day off.

That's why she left me. She told me, Lisa. She told me often. Often enough so it became nagging. And that led to arguments. Constant bloody arguments.

But she was right.

I was full of shit. I still am.

I have lost sight of all of my dreams. To be honest, I can't even recall what those dreams were.

And that would have been fine, except that Lisa didn't. As a consequence, we drifted apart. It was her fault, for not being just like me.

She wanted kids.

I thought I did. Once. I wasn't lying about that.

But I didn't want the responsibility. I didn't want to have to think about school uniforms and shoes, and food in someone else's belly.

We got this place because it had a spare room. I still call it a spare room. Lisa called it the baby's room. It wasn't spare to her.

The antonym for spare is useful. Or required. Or occupied.

And it is occupied and useful, that room. It is most certainly required.

She'd nag me about that most of all. It was the thing we fought over more than any other.

I knew what I was doing. I'm an honest bullshitter, if nothing else.

For as long as the room was occupied and in use, it couldn't be filled with anything else. Such as a child.

Even after I began sleeping on the sofa, it never crossed my mind to clear the room and turn it into a bedroom. It was too risky. It opened a door of opportunity. Nudge that ajar, and it would never be fully closed again.

Besides, there's so much shit in there, it's difficult to open the door wide enough to walk in.

And I'm not that overweight. It's nothing I won't shift from my belly as soon as I make up my mind to do something about it. I'm not that far gone yet. I could do it if I wanted to. I can still jog up the stairs if I have to.

But I don't have to. That's the point.

It's just hard to find the time. What, with work, and life in general.

I'm going to have to get up. Well, I don't have to, but I need the toilet. And Lisa isn't here to wash the bedding any more. Why make work for myself?

Lisa had a biological clock to go with her biological washing powder.

It's different for men. I can have kids when I'm fifty. Sixty, even. Plenty of fucking time. Literally.

I swing my legs free of the covers. My back hurts. Hunched over the screen all last night playing a game. And the night before. And the night before that. And all day at work. It can't be good for you, all that hunching. But it pays the bills.

No gain without pain.

At least I don't smell of oil and grease. Well, only the grease from the chips last night. That's what an education buys you.

I'm dehydrated, a dark yellow puddle sits at the bottom of the bowl. All that beer last night, but this is the result. Where did all the liquid go?

On my belly, I think, as I look down at myself. Navel then feet. That's my view.

Why would Lisa choose to look like this?

And she did. She didn't hang about once she left me. She popped one out within a year. With a wanker called Dave.

At least I still have my hair. Unlike Dave. He shaves his head to make everyone think that he chooses to be bald. Like it's a fucking fashion statement.

I bumped into them in town. I was on my lunch break. He was on paternity leave, pushing the pram.

Lunch only lasts for half an hour. He was lumbered for life.

Yeah, he was proud. But, then, I was proud of my burger. That was why I excused myself. It was going cold.

"Pleasure to meet you," he said.

I just smiled and nodded. No reciprocation, because it wasn't a pleasure to meet him.

Lisa was supposed to have regretted leaving me. She wasn't supposed to be happy.

The kid looked like him. Same hair style.

I'd run the numbers. It was close, but she left me about four weeks before she conceived.

It must have been going on before. They worked together, so...

The work Christmas party would be my guess. She came home drunk as a skunk, reeking of perfume, pino and pernod.

Her short dress rode up as she slumped on the sofa. No bra. Knickers you could floss with.

I felt some need to reclaim her. It was strange, that compulsion. We didn't get very far. She felt sick, and ran to this very toilet.

Without knowing how I got here, I stand at the door to the 'spare' room.

I nudge the door open. Stale air escapes.

The handle hits the exercise bike that I got for myself. Five years ago. I think the digital display shows five kilometers. One a year.

It's there for when I need it. It isn't as though you have to practice. It's like riding a bike. And I could always do that as a kid.

A quarter of a century ago.

It's a tight squeeze through the door.

I hit the button on the digital display on the bike. It does fuck all. A bit like me.

The battery has leaked, oozing a crusty diarrhea substance out of the compartment.

I look at the stacked boxes in the room. All uniform. Thirteen inches by thirteen inches by thirteen inches. Unlucky for some.

Unlucky for me.

There are about a hundred of them, stacked no more than three high.

And not for the first time, I think to myself, "what on earth made my dad think I would be remotely interested in inheriting seven and a half thousand vinyl albums?"

2.

My sisters got the house and all his worldly goods. My brother got the business.

I got this fucking lot.

Hardly fair, thought I to myself. And I may have expressed that sentiment to a few people. Such as my brother and sisters.

I don't express anything to them now. Not since then. All ties are severed.

Dad even went to the bother of stipulating it in his Last Will and Testament. Money was set aside for boxes and transportation, each box numbered, as the collection had to be kept in the order he maintained it on his shelves. In his room. Where he'd spend Sunday afternoons and every evening.

That's what he did when he wasn't working. Well, that and going to record fairs or car boot sales on a Sunday morning. Thereat he'd buy more of this shit.

I almost sold the lot about four years ago. Lisa's nagging was ratcheting up. She claimed to be worried about the weight, and the floor giving way.

They're not that fucking heavy.

I lean down to pick a box up.

They are that fucking heavy.

The delivery company lugged them up here. I was at work. Lisa supervised.

A man Lisa found on the internet came out and had a quick look. He cut the tape and popped the flaps on a few boxes, and made some noises that sounded like he couldn't be arsed being here.

He offered me five grand for the lot, bought unseen. He said something about eighty percent of the value being in just a few of the records. It would take time to sort through them, he said. Besides, condition was everything. They'd need to be visually inspected and play-tested. He didn't appear enamoured at the prospect.

To me, it seemed a bit cheap, that offer. Less than a quid a record. I don't doubt it was about what dad paid for them at the boot sales, but even so. It was my legacy!

So I told the man with the van that I'd think about it. He got a bit pushy at that. Upped his offer to five and a half thousand.

We could have used the money. The car was on its last wheels, and Lisa was looking at a holiday abroad. And then there was the freeing up of the spare room. Lisa had turned thirty-five. I wasn't far behind her.

Apparently, in the dim and distant, I'd suggested it might be a good age at which to procreate. Young enough to have the energy, but old enough to be in a better position financially.

I must have had a few beers when I dreamt that up. I'd forgotten I'd said it. Lisa hadn't.

The holiday abroad was seen as a last hurrah before settling down to parenthood.

The van man got more shirty, muttering on about driving half way across Brakeshire on a weekday evening. He'd go six thousand, if we shook on it there and then. Cash. Off the books.

Lisa was keen. It was a chunk of change.

But something about the man forced me to stall.

"I want to think about it," I repeated, "they were my dad's, so..."

Shrugging, I stopped short of telling a fib about them meaning a lot.

Had I done that, Lisa probably would have pissed herself there and then, in front of the bloke. He might have reduced his offer if she had. Piss staining probably affects the price of such things.

I know that because I bought a Price Guide. He wasn't lying about that, Van The Man. Condition really is everything.

As is the right thing. I thought The Beatles might be worth a lot. And some of it is - the right thing in the right condition. Even the right thing in the wrong condition can be okay. As can the wrong thing in the right condition. But, really, you want to look for the right thing in the right condition.

The wrong thing in the wrong condition is a waste of fucking space.

And I don't doubt that most of what dad bought was exactly that.

The book was my master plan. I'd go through every record in every box, and flog them on the internet. The good stuff, anyway. The fodder could go to... Well, Van Man seemed like the only option.

As I explained it to Lisa at the time, perhaps five hundred of the records were worth bothering with. So, if they had a value of twenty quid each on average, that was ten grand.

The remaining seven thousand could then be flogged off to a dealer, or at car boots, for twenty to fifty pence a pop. Call it another couple of thousand. Anything that didn't sell could go to the charity shop.

I summed it up with, "with a bit of time and effort, I could pull in twelve K. Easy. And that's conservative. It's double the offer we have. Anyway, I didn't like the prick."

So, that was that decided.

I bought the Price Guide, and spent a whole afternoon plucking albums from one of the boxes Van Man had opened, it lying closest to hand at the top of a stack.

It wasn't as easy as I imagined. How the fuck was I supposed to know what was a first pressing? Textured label? Hand-etched run-off groove? I could just about fathom that it was stereo, not mono. And that took me a while.

It smelt old. The paper, and whatnot. The book didn't mention the smell at all.

The condition didn't look too bad, but 'Doesn't Look Too Bad' wasn't an option on the guide to record grading. Ergo, I settled for 'Very Good' as a best fit alternative.

After an hour, I decided that it was probably worth about a fiver, and undoubtedly not worth listing on the internet.

Who's next?

Just deciphering the name of the band and the title of the record was difficult enough. It wasn't very clear. Was 'Kaleidoscope' the band name? No, I deduced, the band was called 'Tangerine Dream', because I found them in the book.

The album 'Kaleidoscope' wasn't listed. Probably worth less than the book qualification value.

I'd seen Van Man stare at that one. His offer of six grand was starting to look generous.

Someone on my gaming group suggested using the internet.

It helped. It had pictures.

That said, it didn't help much. There were so many variations of every release.

The devil, I discovered, was in the detail.

Detail bores me. So does the devil. So, I gave up after three hours spent looking up five records. Well, I didn't give up. I'm no quitter! It would simply have to wait until I had more time to dedicate to the task.

With Lisa having been gone for a year, something tells me that the time might be now.

I should probably put some clothes on first, though.

And I need to eat. And have a cuppa or two. And a dump. Then there's the radio show I like to listen to at eleven. That's about now. There's a live game at half twelve. Another at four.

It's probably not going to be worth starting today. My schedule's filling up. I promised the group I'd log-in at seven for a session. I need to claw some points back after last night. Never play when you've had a few. That should be my motto.

Much to my surprise, I emerge from my bedroom wearing a pair of tracksuit bottoms. They smell a bit stale, having not been worn in... Well, fucking years.

The elasticated waist is tight.

And it's elasticated.

3.

Carting a cup of refreshing cha, and with the radio loud enough to hear up the stairs, I apply myself to the business at hand.

I can see why they call it an exercise bike. It gets you fit enough trying to fucking move it.

It's probably best to use it as a door stop.

The next task is to find something to stop the bleeding. Metal is sharp, I learn. No wonder dad always had scars on his hands.

My initial thought is to take the boxes down stairs one at a time, and sit in front of the telly and do this.

It's not going to happen. It'd be simpler to bring the telly up here. It's a flat-screen, weighing comparatively fuck all.

Ah, but there's no satellite jack up here. If there was, I'd watch telly in bed rather than sit on my reclining chair.

A strange notion washes over me, much like an epiphany, as I understand such things.

I could actually listen to the records!

I'm fairly sure I have a good enough ear to know the good from the bad from the fifty pence box. In addition, I can aurally grade them at the same time, and kill two Byrds with one Rolling Stone.

Dad's record player and other equipment is in the cupboard. He generously left me those, as well, bless him.

Getting to it is my primary concern. It'll involve moving boxes.

The bike is going to have to go in the hallway. If only I could ride it there.

I should probably stop the bleeding before I handle anything. There'll be plasters somewhere. Lisa would have made sure of that. There may even be some antiseptic cream in the bathroom.

It's a bit out of date, but those dates are a con. Everyone knows that.

Back in the spare room, I begin to clear a path.

This could actually be fun, I consider. I quite like music.

As a teenager, I had a few Britpop CDs.

I have no idea what became of them. I replaced the ones I cared about on MP3. I only bothered with a handful, which is probably quite telling.

There were a couple by Blur. But I just downloaded their greatest hits. That's the good stuff. It's all you need. The rest is just filler.

Palmerton Chase, the town of my birth, is famous for being famous for sod all.

It contains no hits. It's all filler.

It's a sleepy little place. It's barely a town, really, and only reached that lofty status once the railway paid it a visit. Before leaving, pronto.

In spirit, it remains a village.

Replete with idiots aplenty.

Close to twenty miles require traversing before Jemford Bridge or Millby are reached. In those places, to some degree, it was possible to buy things. That was where I got my CDs.

I've always liked having access to things. I may not ever take advantage of the amenities, but it's a comfort to know that they're there should I ever wish to.

It's kind of why I miss Lisa.

Anyway, when I left home, I went the whole hog, and moved all the way to Tredmouth on the other side of the county.

It was only forty-odd miles, but it was like another world.

Yeah, worlds apart, dad and I were.

He always had his favourites. And I never was. We didn't share much common ground.

That was why I moved, and the others remained close. The ground at Palmerton Chase suited them, just as it didn't me.

Once I was gone, it was simpler to remain gone.

But the truth is, I stayed away because I didn't want to admit that life wasn't all it might have been.

I didn't want to admit that I might have fucked up.

Staying away sent a message that I didn't need anything. I was hunky-dory, ta very much.

Hunky-dory may, I have an inkling, be the title of an album. Is it in these boxes? Who's it by? Is it any good?

No. If it was any good, I'd know it.

That's the problem with most of these records. I've never heard of them. Who's going to buy records they've never heard of?

Still, even dad must have accidentally picked up some good ones amongst the many. It's the law of averages.

I was an accident. I wasn't planned.

Perhaps, deep down, I was unwanted.

After all, they had the son and heir in my brother, Trev. And they had the girls, in Beth and Yvonne. They were born in that sequence, over a period spanning four years.

There's a seven year gap between Yvonne and myself. Mum and dad were thirty-seven when I entered the world.

I'm more like my mum.

So I'm told.

I don't remember her. Well, very little.

All I recall is a woman who sang, and smelled of paint and varnish. She was an artist.

And the headscarf. I remember that.

It wasn't for religious reasons. It was because the treatment made her hair fall out.

Only through photographs do I know what colour my mum's hair was.

It was the same colour as mine. Fair, but with the grey creeping in by the time we each neared forty. Being fair, it masks it more, and makes us look blonder. Until it dominates. Being bald will disguise it better. I don't suppose that was much solace for mum.

She never quite made it to forty. She died just before that landmark.

I don't recall the two birthdays I spent with her.

But there's a picture of me on my mum's knee. A cake sits in front of me. A single candle smokes, the snap taken just after the flame went out.

I should have been honest with Lisa.

It wouldn't have changed anything. But the truth might have made it easier for both of us.

I didn't want to bring a child into the world, because I was scared of having to leave it in the same way in which I was left.

The thought of getting that attached to anything terrifies me.

4.

"What's the last thing you remember?" the doctor asks me.

"I was moving my exercise bike from the spare room."

She glances at my physique, before adding, "and then you found yourself at the foot of the stairs?"

"That's about the top and bottom of it."

She smiles and writes some notes.

I most definitely would. She's as pretty as a Pretty Thing. I found a record by them in a box after the Van Man came a-calling.

She looks mixed race, but I have no idea of what the mix is made. Asian fusion, I think.

Confusingly, her identity badge informs me her name is Dr. Braun. It sounds Germanic. It's probably her husband's name.

Fuck it. That means she's married. I bet there's a ring under the rubber glove.

To be honest, I'd blown my chances anyway. After all, she's seen me naked.

She inspected all of my body for fractures and the like.

"You don't remember feeling dizzy before you fell?"

"No. I think I remember slipping on the wood floor," I state, "I was wearing some exercise socks, and they were slippery because they'd never been worn before."

I wish I hadn't volunteered the last part.

"You've been lucky, Mr Goods," she tells me, as she shines a light in my eyes that leaves a white streak. It momentarily stops me seeing her clearly. I miss her already.

"Lucky would have been not falling down the stairs," I point out.

She smiles again. "You're badly bruised, that's all. No breaks. We kept you in overnight for observation. That's standard after being unconscious for any amount of time. I'm happy for you to be discharged. Is there anyone we can call to collect you?"

"No. There's nobody, really. I'm single," I drop in, hoping she'll light up and go, 'so am I, we should get together some time.'

Two seconds elapse before I add, "and my family aren't local."

"I'll arrange a ride for you. Do you need any help getting dressed?"

"No, I've been doing it since I was little."

That smile again. I'm winning her over.

She writes and says, "I'm going to give you a prescription for some pain killers. If the pain is unmanageable, contact your GP. Also, no work and plenty of rest for two weeks. And easy on the exercise bike, okay?"

"No problem."

It won't be.

"I've contacted your GP, and he's already notified your place of work, so they're fully aware of what's happened."

"Thank you."

"Any light-headedness, vision problems, severe headaches, you get yourself back here immediately. Is that clear?"

"Understood."

"And rest, Mr Goods. Plenty of rest. You've knocked yourself about, and your body needs time to heal."

I give her a thumbs-up to show that I am on the exact same wavelength. It hurts a bit. I must have banged my wrist.

"And as soon as you feel up to it, make an appointment with your GP. We ran your blood, and found a problem."

Shit.

This is why I didn't want children. This is why.

It's in the genes.

Nodding my understanding, I say, "I know. The C-word, right?"

She nods and smiles her sympathy at me. She almost certainly won't fancy a drink now. Unless she's one of those people that need to be needed. And she could be. She's a doctor, after all. It must be in her nature. A glutton for punishment and pain.

"It's not bad, but your cholesterol is high."

Cholesterol?

She continues as I digest the word, "and there's a risk of stroke, amongst other things. Your GP might decide to put you on some medication. And you may wish to think about your lifestyle. But it sounds as though you're already doing that, with the exercise bike you mentioned."

"Erm, yeah, I knew I'd let myself go a bit. And my diet has been... Well, shit, to be honest. Since Lisa left me. She was my girlfriend. I'm not with her anymore."

"Don't worry. You're okay, but changes need to happen. Particularly as you approach middle age."

She looks at me, and sees an out of shape Approaching-Middle-Age-Man.

I look at her, and see someone I fancy I have a chance with.

One of us is delusional.

It's staggering to discover that they allow delusional people to become medically qualified and work in hospitals.

Yet, my overriding feeling is one of relief.

I don't have cancer.

I'm not like mum, after all.

Shit. Does that mean that I'm actually more like my dad?

5.

It was painful getting up the stairs. My back and legs ache. My breaths are heavy.

I stand staring at the forbidding wall of brown cardboard that fills the spare room.

Black numbers adorn the top of each box. They're roughly in order, so I look for the single digits, and find box number one beneath boxes two and three.

It had to be at the bottom.

An album lasts for, what? Forty minutes. Some of them are doubles, but others will be shorter.

Seven and a half thousand times forty minutes...

I need the calculator function on my phone.

Three hundred thousand minutes.

Fuck me.

Divide by sixty, equals fuck me backwards.

I was hoping to whizz through dad's collection in the two weeks I have off work. I'm going to need five thousand hours.

If I listen to records twenty-four hours a day, seven days a week, it'll take me about seven months to get through them.

I could play them all at forty-five to speed things up.

My idea was to listen for two hours a day. I think I can work that in to my busy schedule. At that rate, it'll take me seven years.

All for ten thousand pounds. If I'm lucky. Van Man was fairly local. Perhaps I should give him a ring.

No. I'm going to do this. I want to do this.

Those are my resolutions; to clear this room, and to get fit and well.

It's agony, sliding the top box off the lower two. It falls and dings a corner. At least the second box can then be slid from one to the other.

Thus, box one is exposed. And box two is ready. Once emptied, box three will be revealed.

I've thought it all through. Anything that sounds and appears interesting and, moreover, valuable, shall be lined up in the hallway leaning against the wall.

The fodder can then be repacked in the boxes as I go through them.

Dad's record player appears to be functioning, insofar as it rotates. The amp has power, and the speakers are hooked up. There was a thingumajig called a pre-amp, but I didn't bother with that. It seemed a bit superfluous and overkill.

Not every minute of every record, I realised, will require listening to. I'm confident I'll know within a minute of the first track starting whether it's a winner or not.

And a website I found may prove useful. It lists artists and their discographies. This is a new word that I have discovered this very day. It's a real word. Each entry has a picture. If you click on the picture, more pictures are available. Labels included.

How hard can this be?

And so I begin a new chapter in my life.

I select the first record from box number one. The handwritten sticker adorning the plastic cover stalls me.

It's in my dad's hand. '00001 - Everly Brothers - Songs Our Daddy Taught Us'.

Rather foolishly, dad inserted the record into the outer protective plastic sleeve so that the open side isn't accessible. It's all going to slow down the process.

Sliding the sleeve from the outer, I shake the cover so the inner sleeve emerges. I tug it free. Again, he's put that in with the open edge covered. Daft idiot. Why make work for yourself?

Finally, after two minutes of what can only be described as dicking around, I have the record in my hand.

And it is in my hand, my fingers all over the shiny black bit.

Dad showed me how to hold a record when I was little. I remember that suddenly.

Without warning, it's as if some muscle-memory is triggered.

"Hold it by the edges, son. Or place your thumb on the edge, and arc your fingers over so they touch the centre label."

My hands weren't large enough back then. I could only do it by the edges.

"That's it! And now put it on the platter, so the spike goes through the hole. Not so easy, is it, eh? It takes practice."

With the record situated, I set the table turning.

"Always give it a helping hand. Overcome the inertia. It'll stop your belt stretching, and your motor burning out."

He could have been describing me, and what I've become.

Round and round it goes, as I bring the arm over.

Bending, I take an age lining it up with the drop zone - that shinier uncut run of vinyl that reflects the light from the window better than the rest of the disc.

Leaning over the record, I see my own face looking up at me. It's indistinct, the black somewhat hiding the detail. A small pulse warps my image on every rotation, despite the record appearing flat.

And in the nebulous distortion, I see myself for the first time in a long time.

I don't like what I see.

I shall be thirty-nine in a couple of weeks time.

Like this record, I've been pointlessly turning over and over. Going through the motions. Being driven by something unseen that lies beneath.

Stretching forward, I allow my visage to become hidden by the purple label. Only the fatness of my neck remains.

I'm ugly.

That's the thought that washes through me.

Pulling away in disgust at my own image, I lower the tonearm.

Slowly it drifts down - floating, as though it's having to fight through some invisible barrier in order to make contact.

I'm quite chuffed with myself for having remembered to remove the dust cap.

The point of the needle - the point of my dad's life, it feels like - makes contact.

I was unknowingly holding my breath.

The groove draws it in, just as I draw in air without which I will cease to be.

And not a sound emanates from the speakers.

Fuck it.

6.

It turns out that I do require the pre-amp.

Once hooked in, I repeat the process, and watch the tonearm and stylus descend.

I know the terminology. My dad taught me. He did it when I was young, and at my most malleable.

He did it before I was old enough and arrogant enough to think I knew everything.

With that arrogance came a rigidity.

A click and a slight scrape accompany the contact, until the needle finds the groove and quietens.

A warm crackle is the introduction. And then a guitar, I think. Acoustic, picked and strummed.

And then two heavenly voices that you just know have been singing together since they were children. Moreover, they were singing these songs back when they were at their most malleable.

I didn't expect any of this. I certainly didn't expect to instantly like the music. In all honesty, I'd anticipated detesting it.

It's folk music. I've never listened to folk music in my life. Folk music is old man's music.

But it sounds like the soundtrack to my on-line gaming, as I lay my money down.

Christ above! I think the next track is about murdering his girlfriend. I can relate to that.

Now they're singing about cheating and leaving me lonely. Lisa must have heard this one.

If I'm to get through these, I should be playing the next record. But I can't stop it. I'll just play the one side.

My back hurts, standing in one position for too long. The floor isn't too inviting. I'll have trouble getting up again if I sit there.

I find myself, as a result, sitting on the bike in the hall. My feet rest on the pedals.

Silver haired daddy of mine and turning back the pages of time.

A line about mother waiting in heaven.

Again, the next track is about mum and dad, and putting shoes on my feet and gloves on my hands.

Before I know it, side one is finished.

I sit motionless on the bike. I honestly can't fathom what just took place.

The record rotates pointlessly, the music exhausted. The stylus buffers at the centre, making a rhythmic ba-bump thirty-three and a third times every minute.

One hundred times I listen to the sound. I count them. And without being aware of it, my feet are pushing on the pedals, and the cycle of the exercise bike turns at exactly the same speed.

How can I have never heard any of these songs before?

Perhaps I did. Dad might have played it countless times.

I dismount, and turn the record over, only touching the edges with my palms and fingers.

Before I can reach and reseat myself on the bike, the music begins. I hold the sleeve, and pore over the writing on the back.

The first thing it tells me is that the record is a collector's item.

I don't care. It's the very first in my dad's collection, and I'm keeping it. If I only keep one, it will be this one. Something to remember him by.

With every word devoured, even the small print informing me that it was made in England, I resume my gentle pedalling.

I listen.

It's a long time since I simply listened.

Dad used to say that we had two ears and one mouth. We were supposed to listen twice as much as we talked.

She kissed her baby boy and then she died, Don and Phil Everly sing to me.

There's something wrong with my vision. Everything is smudged. The doctor warned me about this.

It must be the pain killers, I think, as I rub the heels of my hands into my eyes, blink in a flurry, and reset.

7.

The record won't go back in the sleeve. It's as though it's trying to tell me something.

I peer in to check for any hindrance.

There, at the very back, is a piece of paper.

Reaching my hand in, I snag it between two fingers and draw it out.

I don't recognise my dad's writing at first. Only as I begin to read, do I understand that he penned it.

And that he wrote it to me.

'Hello Danny.

Surprise!

Well, if you're reading this, I must be dead.

If you aren't Danny, then please don't read this. It is of no importance or relevance to anyone but my son. And if he chooses not to discover and read these notes, then he will not have embraced the thing that has given me so much pleasure during my life. I will have misjudged him.

Son, I dare say you may have been disappointed to inherit my vinyl. But don't be. It is the most precious thing I have in my life, along with you children.

Only your mother was more important to me than my music. And when she died, Danny, the music was the thing that kept me going. It kept me sane, and, to some degree, it kept me alive.

I'm sorry if any of that upsets you. But I have made a promise to myself that I shall be completely honest in these letters. Yes, there's more than one.

It wasn't that I didn't love you children enough, but I was so terribly depressed. Every time I looked at you -

especially you - I saw your mum. And it broke my heart all over again. Every single day.

People always think you're like your mum, and physically, you are. But underneath, you're not so different to me.

You weren't planned, you know? You were a shock, to say the least. But a very pleasant one.

Your mum said you were a miracle!

My dearest wish is that you could have known her better. Hopefully, through these letters, you may get to know her a little more.

Myself, too. You might get to understand me. And I hope that, if you do, you'll forgive me for not being all of the father I might have been.

Hey, now listen - this is very important. Don't be sad about me dying.

I've had my life.

And the truth is, a chunk of me died along with your mum all those years ago.

From now on, I'll use her name - Paula.

She was named after a character in a Thomas Hardy novel. Did you know that? I can't remember which bloody book. But she definitely was. I never even knew there was a Hardy character called Paula. It sounds a bit modern.

Anyway, if this has gone to plan, you should have discovered this note in an Everly Brothers album called 'Songs Our Daddy Taught Us'.

It was the first album I ever bought, long before I met Paula. And this is that copy.

I turned fifteen in 1958. Albums were bloody expensive, I can tell you that. I saved and saved for weeks, working as an apprentice car mechanic as soon as I left school. I think an album back then was about a third of my weekly wage. Something like that, anyway.

Combined with Christmas and birthday money, I finally had enough, and rode my bike over to Millby. I knew which record I wanted before I even set off.

I strutted in, clad in my jeans and checked shirt, cocky as you like, and asked for the latest Everly Brothers album.

It was handed to me, and I was invited to give it a play in the listening booth. I declined. I didn't need to do that. I knew my music. I was a man who knew what he wanted from the world.

I paid and left, and rode the twenty miles home, a bag banging against my shoulder blade.

In the door I flew, up to my room, and the power on. There wasn't much power. All I had was a small record player with an inbuilt speaker. The sound was tinny and weak, but it was mine.

On the record went, volume as high as I dared. And I daren't touch it, because it cut out if you did. A loose wire I'd been meaning to solder.

The record span, and the music came out.

And I hated it.

I grabbed the cover and looked at the track listing in horror. There were none of the songs that I knew. Where was 'Bye-Bye Love' and 'Wake Up Little Susie'?

What was all this folk and country rubbish?

I had an urge to take it back, Danny, but I was too proud and embarrassed. Besides, it was a bloody long way to cycle.

But here's the thing. Over the years, I've come to love this record. A year or two on, and I'd get the other Everly Brothers album released in 1958, the one with the hits on. The one I meant to buy that day. But I never liked it as much as this one.

Strange, isn't it? I had an expectation that stopped me listening and appreciating it at the time.

We all do that, I think, in life.

Those old folk tunes they sang so beautifully on 'Songs Our Daddy Taught Us', would open my ears to much more of a similar ilk come the sixties.

I think this album is ahead of its time, son. And it took me a little while to catch up to it.

It's in near mint condition, a testament to how little I played it prior to getting a much better turntable in the early-sixties.

It's worth about fifty pounds. With inflation, that's probably less than I paid for it. There was wear and tear on the bike to be considered. And to my ego.

The record I intended buying that day is worth about ten to fifteen pounds, I believe.

But that isn't really the point.

Appreciate what you have, not what you don't. And keep an open ear to go with an open mind.

Don't worry, I haven't put a note in every record. Only in the ones that have a story attached to them. It may not be worth telling, but it's the story of my life.

Every moment, good and bad, is contained within the grooves on these records.

A song can trigger a memory that I would otherwise be incapable of recalling. They act as a prompt, and as a storage device.

This album was my starting point, and the rest are numbered and stored in the order in which I discovered them.

I wish we'd done this face to face, but I was never very good at communicating in that way. Paula knew it about me. She used to say that I communicated my true feelings to her through the records I played. She knew my mood from what I was listening to.

She was the only person who could ever read me, and the only soul on this earth to ever truly know me.

But she's long gone, and I'm glad you're here with me now.

I'll catch you soon.

Love, Dad.'

8.

It's tempting to rummage through the box and find the next note.

There's no hurry. Everything I do, even my thoughts, are always so rushed. I lurch from one thing to the next, and never fully embrace anything as a result.

As he wrote, 'appreciate what I have.' And I have him in these one hundred boxes. The essence of the man is held in seven and a half thousand vinyl records.

If it takes me years, I will do this.

Hopefully, through that, I'll also come to know my mum. Perhaps I'll even get to somewhat fill the gap that has left me with a hollow core for as long as I can remember.

For my whole life, it's felt as though there isn't quite enough oxygen in the air.

Thus, I play on.

'00002 - Gene Vincent - Gene Vincent Rocks And The Blue Caps Roll'.

'00003 - Eddie Cochran - Singin' To My Baby'.

I sit in the hallway, gently rotating the pedals on the bike, and forget about my pain.

I forget to eat and drink.

Even Lisa is forgotten.

Before I know it, it's dark outside. My gaming group has long since started. Without me.

I don't care. I don't care about anything but this.

The values surprise me. The Gene Vincent and Cochran LPs are worth a couple of hundred each.

They're all immaculate. Dad really did look after his records.

I remember the telling off I got for mishandling one. I was probably eight or nine, and had snuck into dad's room unbidden.

His arrival startled me, as he snapped, "what are you doing?"

The tonearm fell from my fingers, as I attempted to play a record in the careful way he'd shown me.

An awful bump and scrape screeched from the speakers.

For the life of me, I can't recall what the record was. But I liked it, and wanted to hear it. Hence my sneaking into the room and helping myself.

It reminded me of mum. It contained a refrain about her hair, and it made me smile at her because she didn't have any.

She sang it to me when I was teething, and she'd shake and rattle a toy in time with it.

That was why I had such an urge to hear it. One of those same teeth had worked loose and fallen out.

"Watch what you're bloody well doing!" dad barked at me.

I tried to lift the stylus from the rotating disc, but I was so nervous, I dragged it painfully across the surface.

"Leave it! Get out!" I was ordered.

I ran from the room.

Did I ever go back? Certainly not on my own, and perhaps not even when dad was present. That was the point at which it ended, the hanging out together in his room.

What was the record? It must be in these boxes somewhere, so I have to come to it.

Fish. It was something about fish.

A sad smile stretches my cheeks.

Prior to the day when I dropped the needle, I'd spend hours sitting in dad's room with him as he played his records.

I'd sit and draw, or play a game, and absorb the sounds by osmosis.

We didn't converse much. Dad wasn't a talker, as his letter stated.

From time to time, as a thought occurred to him, he'd tell me something relating to the record he was playing. I didn't really comprehend. And by the age at which I was able to understand, I was no longer interested.

They were just dad's stories, that he told over and over. It felt as though he had about fifteen of them, that he would trot out. One to crowbar in to any occasion.

My siblings and I would roll our eyes and pretend to listen. Dad was off on one again.

Yet, here I am eagerly anticipating the second letter. I can't wait to read the next tale.

Is it the same thing as dad experienced with 'Songs Our Daddy Taught Us'? Was I simply not mature enough to appreciate what he was saying?

Life is so simple when we're young. We know everything. And what we don't know isn't worth knowing.

'00014 - Ray Charles - 'What'd I Say?'.

The record is already playing before I peer inside the sleeve and discover two envelopes.

9.

One is sealed, the other torn across the top.

The open one has dad's name and an address on the front. It's an address in Palmerton Chase that I recognise as being where my grandparents lived long before I was born.

A new brick bungalow, with a backdrop of the Brake Hills, is my only vague memory of a place they called home.

The stamp adheres to the envelope, and is franked from Drescombe, a town about ten miles to the southwest.

Handwritten in blue ink, I instinctively know the writing is a woman's.

Is it my mum's?

Am I holding something that she held? Is her saliva on the dry glue strip...

No. This was long before they met. The franking date is February 12th, 1960.

Two days before Valentine's Day, it occurs to me.

Should I be looking? Did dad forget that this one was here? It feels like an intrusion.

Gingerly, I slide the contents out. There's a letter from my dad, along with two cards.

'Hello again, son.

How are you getting on with the records? It's all rock'n'roll up to this point, but I was beginning to broaden my scope.

I first heard about the title track, and the name Ray Charles, because of Eddie Cochran. I saw him and Gene Vincent in Sheffield just a few days before Valentine's Day in 1960.

It was the first big concert I ever attended. It was also the best. Nothing would ever match up to that night.

But, as with a lot of things, I didn't appreciate it until I had a few points of comparison.

At the time, and in the moment, I believed every performance I would ever attend would be at least as good. As a consequence, I've spent the rest of my life regretting not paying more attention.

Furthermore, I thought I would see Eddie and Gene on stage again. I never did. Two months on, and Cochran was dead. He was just twenty-one, Danny.

At the concert that evening in Sheffield, I met a girl. She'd travelled from Drescombe on the train, just as my mate and I had done from Palmerton Chase.

We encountered one another on the platform as we made our way home.

I lost my virginity that night, son.

Looking back, I put it down to adrenaline and excitement. I was sixteen, soon to be seventeen, and we were buzzing after the show. She flattered me, and said how I looked a bit like Eddie Cochran. I didn't. But I wanted to.

She wore this yellow dress that clung to her curves, with a matching yellow headband through her dark brown hair. And white shoes. I remember that. It's funny, the things you remember. Her name was Mags. Short for Margaret.

It was clumsy and awkward, as we did it in a compartment on the train. My mate kept watch outside the door.

It didn't last long.

We sat the rest of the journey holding hands. And before we left the train at Palmerton, her destination being one stop on, I wrote my name and address on the programme from that night, and gave it to her.

How I wish I'd kept that programme!

But it didn't matter in the moment, because I'd get another one next time. There would always be a next time, right?

Ah, I must share the truth with you. I've wanted to tell someone about this since the day it took place, but was silenced by a foolish shame.

Again, I reason that if you're reading this, then I'm dead, so it's of no consequence. It's a confession of sorts, and I am contrite. I have been for half a bloody century.

I had a girlfriend at the time, Danny. Her name was Helen. She was beautiful. A petite little blonde, with a perfect figure, and - most importantly - a smart and sharp brain.

Believe me, I would have ended up marrying Helen Clancy.

You probably don't want to read that. And, of course, I'm glad I didn't, because I would never have married Paula. And all four of you kids wouldn't have been born.

The right result came about from the wrong decisions.

Ha, it's funny how often that seems to be the way of life.

So, I loved Helen.

But I wanted sex.

It was that simple. Mags, the girl on the train, wasn't a patch on Helen. Not even close. But she was prepared to offer something that Helen wasn't ready for.

I'd tried it on, Danny, but I didn't want to pressure her, or make her do something she'd regret.

So I ended up doing something that I've regretted ever since.

Valentine's Day fell on the Sunday that year, and I bought this Ray Charles record in Millby on Saturday, February 13th.

I know the time and place, and I know what it cost me.
Both financially, and more broadly.

Mags had told me about the LP on the way home from the
show, and I had to have it. Yes, for the music Eddie
Cochran listened to. But also because Mags had it, and I
naively believed it would bring us closer together and bond
us.

I was infatuated with her. We often are with our first full
lover.

On the Sunday morning, my mother propped two
envelopes against the toast rack when I came down for
breakfast.

She kissed me and held my face so that my cheeks
scrunched. She still saw me as a kid. Parents always do, I
think.

I pushed her away, Danny. I told her to get off and stop
mithering me. I snapped at her.

I did it because I wasn't a kid. I was a big man. I'd seen
Eddie Cochran and Gene Vincent. I had two Valentine
cards. And I'd had sex with a woman on a train.

And now, as I sit here writing this, and know that I'm
nearing the end of my life, I'd give anything - anything! -
for an embrace and kiss from my mum.

I still see the hurt on her face, son. The pain of rejection
was etched on her.

The envelopes were nonchalantly opened as I drank my
tea and chewed on a slice of toast. It was an act. I was
churning inside.

There was the expected one from Helen, which I barely
heeded. Read the words, Danny. I read them over and over
for two years. She loved me. There's no doubt about it.

What do you think Helen meant where she writes, 'roses are red, violets are blue, my heart is yours, claim the rest of me too'?

The other card came from Drescombe. It had to be Mags. She had my address, remember. I never had hers.

She didn't reveal her identity, signing off with a question mark. But it had to be her. I knew no other women in Drescombe, after all.

Helen shrugged it off when I broke up with her that Sunday afternoon. She calmly took my rejection, and stated that it might be for the best. After all, she was hoping to be off to college the following year, and it meant moving away.

Yes, it was probably for the best, all things considered.

But I wasn't that stupid, Danny. I saw how her lip quivered, and her hands shook. She bottled it all up, until she was alone and could let it out. Or so I have imagined countless times.

It was only after she'd gone, that I lay on my bed, slipped my hand beneath the pillow, and found the condom she'd planted there in readiness.

The following day, my sister, your Aunt Patty, gleefully informed me that she'd got a friend to send the other card from Drescombe. It was a joke. A wind-up.

I never heard from Mags. I went to Drescombe to look for her, but didn't find her. I asked around the coffee shops and in the record department in the electrical store, but nobody knew anything about her.

As a result, I've never been in love with this Ray Charles album, despite its undeniable quality.

I play it from time to time, though. I do that to remind myself of a lesson learnt many years ago.

Strangely, when I listen to it, I never think of Mags. I always think of Helen, and what might have been.

I'm haunted by the hurt I caused, rather than any pain inflicted on me.

We're always, I think, drawn to the thing we missed out on, rather than the thing we ever had.

Is it because a thing imagined is better than a thing experienced? Imagined can be perfect. Real life rarely is.

Despite my earlier assertion that Paula was my true destiny, along with all that resulted from the union, this is one of those moments in life. If I could go back, I'd handle it so differently.

Helen never did go to college. Within a few months, she fell pregnant. She began seeing that mate of mine, who I went to the concert with.

I heard, about a year after the events I describe, that she'd moved away to Tredmouth.

I never saw her again.

Well, only occasionally. I picture her in my mind each time I play this Ray Charles record.

I couldn't see what I had, Dan. All I could see, was what I wasn't getting.

Both of the cards I mention are in this record sleeve. You may have spotted another sealed envelope. It contains my card to Helen.

She left that Valentine's Day without ever opening it. It never felt right for me to break the seal. Over time, it became symbolic - the intactness of her that I never got to penetrate.

For the life of me, I can't recall what I wrote. Given the events, it probably wouldn't have been anything too lovey-dovey.

You can open it, if you wish.

I'll leave the decision to you.

Well, that's it. That's my guilty little secret. One of them, anyway.

Thanks for your time, son.

Time is the most precious commodity in life. It's the most valuable thing one person can ever give to another.

I only learnt that after it had slipped through my fingers.

Love, Dad.'

10.

A new day dawns.

No time to waste.

I'm up at first light. Showered, dressed, and fed and watered.

First light isn't saying much. It's February. The sun doesn't bother rising till just after eight.

Lazy old sun.

My aches and pains are easing since my fall. I'm sleeping better. Yesterday, I took a painkiller with breakfast, and didn't touch them until bed time.

I'm too busy. I don't have time for pain.

Mind over matter. No more wallowing. In self-pity or anything else.

My phone went yesterday. It was one of my gaming mates that I've never actually met, seeing why I hadn't logged on for a few days. I made some excuse. I resented the intrusion.

People steal your time, if you let them. They sap your energy, sucking it out of the front of your face.

He asked me what I was up to while I was laid up?

Nothing, I fibbed.

He'd be using the time constructively, if it was him.

"Will you be on-line later?" he asked.

"I doubt it."

"You're falling behind."

"I'm getting ahead." Fuck off.

I didn't say that. But I thought it. I told him I had a doctor's appointment. Better dash. Speak soon. Bye.

My thoughts are rushing at me again. Staccato. Listening to music makes them flow. It elongates them, and slows me down.

No beer for me in three days. I can't drink with the meds. I haven't missed it. I haven't missed any of the things that I used to do.

I certainly haven't missed work.

It's only Wednesday. Three days since the fall. Two since I returned from hospital.

'00017 - Bobby Darin - That's All'.

00018 - Buddy Holly & The Crickets - The Buddy Holly Story'.

'00019 - Eddie Cochran - self-titled'.

'00020 - John Lee Hooker - House Of The Blues'.

Wow! Dad's taste was changing.

'00021 - Billy Fury - The Sound Of Fury'.

On they go. I play them all. No skipping and no ending early. Every track on every side of vinyl is listened to in its entirety. All the while, the pedals turn in time, as I tot up the values in my head.

I wish time would slow down, so I might have more time to listen.

No. I wish time would reverse, and that I could go back.

More hours pass, divided into fifteen to twenty minute segments.

My mind is tranquil.

With a sense of mild shock, it registers that I'm calm and relaxed. There isn't much I care about. A few days ago, I believed I cared about all manner of things.

The truth is, I don't.

Or, rather, if I do, then they are bigger things. They are certainly not materialistic.

I care that I'm alone. But I'm not lonely as I sit here. The loneliness only washes over me when I go to bed at night, and stare unseeing at the inaudible dark, as I wait for sleep to find me.

Eating and drinking are things I resent, but know are required. I partake at times convenient, and forsake convenience food.

The leaning pile of records in the hall - the keepers - far outweigh the ones I intend getting rid of.

In fact, only two are back in the box. One is a soundtrack I didn't care for. The other is by The Chipmunks.

I plough on, not disliking anything that I hear.

'00050 - Howlin' Wolf - Moanin' In The Moonlight'.

Inside which, I find a letter.

11.

'Hello Danny.

Well, you've made it up to 1962. I was nineteen that year. This was my fiftieth record. I'd bought most of them myself, about one a month as I could afford it, but a few were Christmas and birthday presents. You might be able to work out which ones they are!

It's funny, isn't it? People know that you like music, and they assume that you like any music. Hence The Chipmunks.

My aunt got it for me, bless her. I cherish it now because it came from her. She wrote on the back cover, if you look. Merry Christmas, Billy - love from your Aunt Bet.

She was a wonderful woman. As with so many people in my life, I wish you could have known her better.

Aunt Bet was my dad's sister, and she was one of those people who would give you whatever she had. Even her last penny, Danny.

She'd deprive herself, if she thought someone else might appreciate something, or need it more than she did.

Some people are like that. They seem to derive more pleasure from giving than receiving.

Well, I was an ungrateful little sod back then. We all are, I think, at that age.

So, when I opened the Chipmunks album on Christmas morning, my Aunt Bet sat watching me eagerly, I pulled a face, and muttered something disparaging about, "what would I want with that crap?"

My old man gave me a clip round the ear for being so bloody ungracious. And he was correct to do that.

I felt bad right away, and apologised, but the hurt was done.

By way of atonement, I suppose, I played it that Christmas morning. It was the first record I ever played on my new hi-fi system mum and dad had helped me buy.

Oh, the sound from that system, Danny!

It was housed in a wooden cabinet, and had two whole speakers. Two!

We all sang along to the album - 'Old MacDonald', 'Three Blind Mice', 'Whistle While You Work', 'Pop Goes The Weasel'.

At the end came 'The Chipmunk Song (Christmas Don't Be Late)', and I danced around the front room with my lovely Aunt Bet, and prayed that it wasn't too late.

We laughed and laughed until our faces ached, Danny!

Those are the best moments in life, you know? Those unplanned times that just happen along when our expectations are low.

Always look out for them. Keep 'em peeled, son.

As soon as it's planned, a degree of pre-emptive thought comes into play. More often than not, the reality will fail to match up.

Until you kids came along, that was my best Christmas. The Chipmunks were on repeat, and everyone was so happy.

It was also the last Christmas I spent at home with my parents.

Come the June of 1962, and I'd have my own place.

My Aunt Bet got me the record because of the label. She was so eager to please, and she'd seen me looking at records on the London imprint - Eddie Cochran or The Everly Brothers - and so she went out and tried to find me another.

Okay, so, why is this letter in a Howlin' Wolf album, and not in the Chipmunks LP? Good question, son.

Well, Aunt Bet being Aunt Bet, decided to get me another record she couldn't really afford - one I would appreciate.

The second record I played on my new hi-fi, was a John Lee Hooker album that you've already come across. I announced I was getting into the blues.

I only had that one blues LP. Ray Charles didn't really count.

So, as a flat-warming gift six months on, she presented me with this album.

I'd never seen it, and had never heard of the record or the artist.

But I knew from the cover that I was going to love it.

And I did.

It changed my life, and pointed to most of what would follow. And I'm not just referring to the music.

The main reason I'd never come across it in my vinyl hunting, was because it had never been released in the UK. It was an American import.

The question was - how on earth did my aunt get hold of it?

After all, this was Brakeshire. Had it been London or Liverpool, it might have made sense. She lived in Palmerton Chase, the same as me. There was nowhere in the county where blues imports were to be had, to the best of my knowledge.

But Aunt Bet knew a man.

Alistair McIntyre was the man in question. Everyone knew him as Ally Mac.

He lived in a rambling house midway between Drescombe and Millby. I'd cycled past his place every time I'd ventured to Millby to buy vinyl, and never once imagined what might lie within that stone walled boundary.

Ally Mac had spent most of the fifties in prison.

He'd served seven years for repeatedly beating a man who dared to steal from his father, Chas.

Just after the Second World War, I learnt that my Aunt Bet had gone on a few dates with Ally.

She was a confirmed spinster by the time I was old enough to know about such things, so the revelation came as a bit of a shock.

Anyway, it hadn't worked out between them, but they'd parted on good terms, and were still close friends.

Ally Mac is the most terrifying person I ever met, son.

He was also one of the most generous and caring men I would encounter in my life.

All he asked for was loyalty and integrity.

In prison, he met a man. That man was Baz Baxter. He was serving a stretch for tax fraud. The word was that he was set up by his accountant, but he did his time without complaint.

Baz was a builder and property developer, and he owned most of the clubs in Tredmouth that were worth going to.

He was keen to book music acts to perform in those clubs, and Ally Mac, thanks to a contact he'd made during the war, knew a London based agent who could supply them.

Ally would be the middle man. He was already into the jukebox business in the county's pubs and clubs, so it was a logical next step.

As a result of all of that, Ally Mac had the most amazing house I've ever set foot in.

Classic jukeboxes stood in every nook and cranny. In what was once a library, he had floor to ceiling wood shelving that bowed under the weight of more records than I'd ever seen in one place in my life.

It honestly felt as though every record ever released was in that room. And there were multiple copies of many, as agents and promoters from all over the world sent him records by way of promotion.

Down in the cellar and servants quarters, were an uncountable number of slatted wooden crates containing tens of thousands of seven inch singles for the jukeboxes.

I could have spent the rest of my life going through them, and not reached the end.

Indeed, it was the scale of it that repointed me towards albums. Singles were never my thing. I loved the artwork that came with an LP, and the slower speed at which it rotated. My desire was to sit and absorb the music, not to be up and down turning from side to side.

Thanks to Aunt Bet, I hooked up with Ally Mac.

You'll remember him from when you were a kid.

Though, by then, of course, she was calling herself Alisha.

I'd fix his cars in those early-sixties, and he'd pay me in records. An awful lot of the records that follow this one were picked from Ally Mac's shelves.

Later, after I set up my own garage, I'd get the contract to service and maintain the fleet of vehicles both he and Baz Baxter used to ferry bands, musicians, equipment and promoters around.

Those contracts kept the business afloat, Danny. I'm not sure I'd have survived the seventies without them.

Everything came about because of the records, son. That's the point of this. Every important act to constitute the dramatic performance that is my life, can be directly linked back to a record.

Each of the actors playing their parts, were met similarly.

The first time I knocked on Ally Mac's door, he opened it wearing a spangly ball dress, with a feather boa around his neck. He was the first man I ever saw wearing make-up, and I was tempted to run for my life.

But he was never untoward or improper. In fact, he always liked women, not men. Hence his dating of Aunt Bet. Later, after he rechristened himself Alisha, he claimed to be a lesbian.

"You must be William," he said, offering me a soft-skinned but firm hand to shake.

"That's right. Bill," I clarified.

"Bethany's nephew."

I nodded. It sounded right, but I didn't know that was her actual full name.

He carried on, "because of that, you're welcome here. Until you aren't. But that's up to you. Act like a cunt, and I'll treat you like a cunt. Fair enough?"

I nodded.

"You work on cars, correct?"

Again, I nodded.

"And you like records?"

"Er, yes. I do."

"See that 1961 Chevrolet Impala there?"

"The red one with the white stripe?"

"That'll be it. Two thousand miles on the clock, and the piece of shit won't start. Have a shufty, will you? Fix that, and I reckon it's worth two albums of your choosing. Do we have a deal, Bill?"

We did. It was a dodgy battery. I had it switched out and purring in a jiffy.

"Pop round every other week, if you like," Ally suggested, "and keep the motors ticking over for me. Can you do that?"

And so it began.

All because of a bloody Chipmunks record!

As I was leaving on that first day, sat in my black 1955 Ford Anglia 100E - my first car! - he leaned in the window.

Being June, he'd changed into a loose blouse and an A-line skirt that hung to just below his knees.

Two records sat in the footwell on the passenger side.

"Thanks for today," he said amiably.

"Pleasure. Thank you," I said, and offered him my hand.

"Do you think it's weird that I wear ladies clothes?" he asked without warning, my hand clenched tightly in his, as though he could feel the honesty in my answer through it.

I didn't snap an answer. I paused and thought. He saw that.

"It's unusual," I answered, "but if it makes you happy, I see nothing wrong with it. It's your business, and I don't see how it could be hurting anyone else."

"Good lad. Honest, that was. I like that. Ever upset your aunt again, and I'll break your fucking neck. Clear?"

I nodded that it was crystal clear. There was no doubt that he could and would.

With that, he released my hand, span in military march fashion, and strode back to his house.

I drove home shaking like a leaf.

It's hard to say what made Ally so terrifying. There was a supreme confidence about him, and a hardness in his eyes and manner that was flint like. He had an air of being prepared and willing to do whatever it would take. I always thought of him as being like a drill, that would go through anything if it had to.

Never judge a book by its cover, Danny. And never judge a record before you've played it.

And whenever anybody gives you anything with good intentions, be grateful and respectful.

Take it from an old man.

I'll catch you soon, pal.

Love, Dad.'

Before heading downstairs to make a cup of tea, I retrieve the Chipmunks album, and add it to the growing mound I intend to keep.

At the same time, I alter my intention. It probably makes more sense to put the records I'm keeping back in the boxes. The others can go in the hall.

That way I can get to my bedroom.

'South Pacific' stands all alone, bothering nobody.

12.

I don't have these stories. They don't exist in my life. There are no characters that spring to mind, whose tales are worth telling.

Is it generational?

Born in 1980, the time I went to secondary school was the period when I think things began to change.

Very seldom are the times I recall being told no. There were no completely wrong answers.

At home, I was destined to be the baby. And there was sympathy I could always exploit because of mum dying when I was so small. And I did exploit it.

It led to me being what I am. Spoiled, I suppose. And entitled.

Life-experience wasn't anything sampled. It was something done virtually, for which there are very few consequences.

I alter my course each time I encounter an obstacle in life. I walk away and hide when faced with any hurdle, because even the smallest hurdle is seen as insurmountable. I resent its presence. It shouldn't be there.

My inclination is to stop, and wait for someone to remove it.

Everything I do, I play at. There's no commitment or ability to see things through to a finale.

Up to now.

I'm reflective. The combination of reading about dad's life, and tying it in to my own, has resulted in me staring at nothing. There is nothing reflecting back of my own existence.

When I die, and I shall, there is nothing to leave that is worth having. There are no tales to tell. There are no children to folklorically continue my life experiences, or inherit any legacy.

There is no such legacy pertaining to me.

But I knew these characters from the past. I remember Ally Mac. He'd sit silently, scarily, observing. He would say very little, and when he did speak, it was concise, as he either sought information, or imparted it.

He wasn't large, unlike Baz Baxter who was a block of a man, with his saddle-bag cheeks and big toothy grin. And even after he became Alisha, he maintained a strong masculinity in his features. The curly wig he wore wouldn't soften him to an extent that you could take him for a woman.

Ally Mac gave me the impression of a man who was constantly thinking. The problem was, to look at him, it seemed that his mind was always occupied by thoughts of violence. I don't recall ever seeing him laugh. He'd smile. He'd ask how I was, and grin with his mouth. But there was no mirth in the rest of his face.

That said, I always liked him. Or her. And she was good to me as a nipper. There was always money slipped into my hand, or easter eggs sent, and birthday and Christmas gifts delivered.

Still, a metal coldness was always present in Ally Mac.

I know what dad meant when he likened Ally to a drill. To observe him-her, I imagine that high-pitched whirring is what she heard in her head constantly.

These records are mine now. As are the memories contained within them. Well, the ones dad deemed important enough to pass on.

Thanks to him, I do possess something worth having.

Granted, they are not my memories, but they are my history - my legacy. Because legacy is a double-entendre. It's heritage as well as inheritance. It's tradition and history, just as much as it is something to bequeath.

History was always something that seemed redundant. From the nineties onwards, the future was the focus, a shiny digital world that lay ahead. And not the staid crusty world from before.

Nobody of my peer group 'collected' anything. We accumulated, but did not collect. The closest I have to a collection, are the old computer games and equipment that get tossed into the cupboard beneath the television.

All I have, is a collection of cables.

I'll never revisit any of it. There are no memories attached, or sentiment involved. They were replaced by something newer and, therefore, better.

'00051 - Dave Brubeck Quartet - Time Out'.

'00052 - Dave Brubeck Quartet - Time Further Out'.

Are these the two albums dad got that day at Ally Mac's? They must be. They're a departure from the rock and blues that dad has to this point. Were they his choice, or did Ally Mac steer him towards them?

What did he make of them? There's no note explaining.

I love them. Two of the tracks on the first one are vaguely familiar. The drums are immense.

There's something incredibly cool about the music, even now, in the present day. And they're nearly sixty years old.

Dad would listen to jazz often. He once said that it relaxed him. Jazz and blues were his way of unwinding. Along with a bit of Sam Cooke and Ray Charles. Dad adored Sam Cooke.

Both are represented, as I play my way through 1962. As are Bob Dylan, Bo Diddley, Del Shannon, Lightnin' Hopkins, B.B. King, Tornadoes.

'00077 - John Barry - Dr. No'.

I've seen the film. The main theme is as good as any there's ever been.

Devouring the notes on the sleeves, I see the shift, as dad began buying more British music as 1962 ended and 1963 dawned.

I know enough to know that The Beatles would have been breaking around the time. And they changed everything.

Dad was so eclectic in his music taste.

For myself, I've always stuck with the music that soundtracked my teenage years. I never looked back, in anger or otherwise, and rarely paid attention to anything beyond 'my' time.

Music became something that was there in the background. It always accompanied another activity. It was like a sauce or a side salad, where all the attention is on the main event - the steak, I suppose.

Dad would sit alone in his room, and listen through headphones by the time I reached double figures. The television was always blasting out, so it was the only way he could properly hear.

I haven't watched television since Saturday night. I have no idea what's going on in the world. No news has reached my ears.

No news is good news. It's good news week.

I don't miss it, all of that input - the filling of every second of every day, with information and 'news' that didn't really apply to me. It was always somebody else somewhere else. Yet, somehow, I'd find myself attaching myself to it. I'd take it personally, and become anxious as a result.

Anxious on behalf of unknown others.

Who cares about me?

It scared me, when I fell down the stairs.

I lied to the paramedics and the gorgeous doctor about being unconscious. I was awake all the while.

And I did feel a dizziness before I fell. I fibbed about that, too.

The hangover, and not eating properly, and lack of sleep all played a part, I don't doubt. And, yes, the cholesterol was a factor, I'm sure.

My hand found the bannister, and my exercise socks did slip, but I was too weak to prevent myself from falling. Too out of shape.

I didn't possess the strength to hold myself up.

So I lay there in the dark, wondering if I was dead.

I called out. I called for Lisa. Instinct.

Almost, I called for my mum.

Fucking stupid.

And my dad.

Just as fucking stupid.

Nobody came, obviously. Because there was nobody I could call on.

My phone was in my pocket.

Who you gonna call?

I tabbed through and hit Lisa's mobile number. And she answered.

"I've fallen down the stairs."

"Have you broken anything?"

"I don't think so."

"Can you move?"

"Yes. I think I can get up."

"Have you phoned for an ambulance?"

"No. Not yet. I rang you first."

"Why?"

Her question stalled me. I had no answer. "I don't know."

"What do you want me to do?"

I didn't reply. How could I tell her that I wanted her to come over and take care of me?

"Look, I have to go," she said somewhat tetchily.

"Sorry. I shouldn't have phoned you."

"No, you shouldn't. You should have phoned an ambulance, Dan."

"I think I'm okay."

"I have to go. The baby's crying."

The only crying baby was me.

I dialled 999.

As I sat at the foot of the stairs, and waited for the ambulance to arrive, I had a dreadful feeling at my core.

I was utterly petrified of being alone when my time came.

13.

'00100 - The Beatles - Please Please Me'.

'Hello Danny son.

How are you getting on?

Here's something you may not know about me. I was never the biggest Beatles fan. I remember you'd listen to them quite a bit in the mid-nineties. It was because of Oasis, I think. That was what got you into their later LPs.

I didn't dislike them at all, and I have all of their UK albums.

Indeed, this is a gold label Parlophone stereo version, that I know I bought in late April of 1963. It was purchased in a long-since defunct shop in Tredmouth.

Ally Mac had sent me over in a van to deliver a jukebox to the shop. It specialised in high-end audio equipment, and offered a very select few albums - usually jazz, as well as stereo versions of other music.

Had I liked them more, I probably would have picked up a mono copy prior to then. Thus, by fluke, I ended up with the rarer record.

Values have never much interested me, because I knew I would never sell them. To me, they were priceless.

But it was inevitable that, occasionally, I'd see a record in a shop, and the price tag attached. And I'd know I had that very same edition.

From time to time, I'd pick up a music magazine, and see a discography that revealed some of the values.

As I say, it was irrelevant to me.

You may have sold them all, for all I know. If so, that's your choice. They are yours to do with as you please. Don't keep them to please please me!

As I've aged, I can see it was wrong of me to expect you to be interested in the same things as I was. You are your own person, Danny. An individual.

As long as you're happy, I don't care about anything else.

That was all I ever wanted for any of you, you know? Happiness.

I simply wanted you all to make the best lives for yourselves that you could.

Those opportunities weren't so readily available to me. I left school at fifteen, and went to work. I carried on working until I was physically incapable of doing so. Had I been able, I would have carried on until the day I died. Only my failing health forced me to stop.

What a waste of life, Danny! I admit it. There you go. Even after Paula died, I didn't back off. In fact, I worked harder than ever, and spent more hours there. I did that to block it all out.

And when she was ill and dying, I went to work rather than spend every second I could with the love of my life.

Beneath a car in the workshop, I could pretend none of it was real.

Only when I emerged did it become a reality, and something I had to deal with.

I hid, son.

I justified my behaviour by preaching about responsibility and work ethic, and all that garbage. At the time, I actually believed what I was saying.

Work sets you free? No, son. It makes a slave of you.

And I was lucky! I genuinely enjoyed tinkering around with cars and engines. At least I wasn't stuck in a job that I hated.

I know how much you enjoy your work, son. But if you ever tire of it, then change it. And don't let it control your life.

Work out how much money you need to live a full life you've defined for yourself, and do only as much as that requires.

That's my advice.

And if you choose to sell these records to help enable that, then good for you.

It made me hard, Danny, when your mum died. I'm not sure it's the right word. Not hard. I was never that. But it made me a bit of an emotional void.

That was the only version of me you have memory of. The others can recall the man from before, I think. They can overlook somewhat, and, as a consequence, be more understanding.

I think you lost both of your parents at that time, Danny.

Afterwards, you only ever saw the lesser mono version of me.

With Paula by my side, I was full stereo, with a bright gold label and shiny pristine vinyl!

I was worth more.

I had a greater value.

My mind was closed to moving on. I would always be loyal to Paula. And nobody after ever came close.

Paradoxically, I never attached myself to any one music scene, or any one band.

I didn't really collect any artist. There were some who, if I saw it, I'd get it. But my aim was to sample as much music as possible, from a variety of different genres.

Country music never did much for me, I will concede. But everything else was indulged in and enjoyed.

Life was like that in general. I had my own place, a car, a steady job and a trade. I had money in my pocket. It was a fantastic time to be alive. And to be young was the icing on the cake. I felt so free. I got to grow up through and with the best of music ever. From the rock'n'roll revolution as a teenager, to the colourful creative brilliance of the sixties, as it morphed from jazz, folk and blues, to beat and garage and psychedelia. On through prog, early electronic, rock and punk.

The problem with it all, is that, come the new millennium, I'd heard and seen it all before. Just about everything that came thereafter was derivative.

Don't get me wrong, I still enjoyed music from that period. But nothing sounded as fresh and exciting as it once had. I could always pick out at least one point of reference and influence.

Perhaps, though, that was just me getting old and stale.

Psst, Danny - do you want to know a secret?

I thought The Beatles 'Please Please Me' was derivative when I first heard it!

Don't tell anyone.

Till next time,

Dad.

PS - I love you.'

14.

The replacement computer arrived for the exercise bike. '00115 - Françoise Hardy - self-titled' accompanies the installation. It's a French pressing. I guess it came from Ally Mac's shelves.

Earlier today, I had the supermarket deliver my groceries. Cereals, fruit, vegetables and whole grain bread formed the bulk of the order, along with fish and healthy option frozen pasta dishes.

I've been looking it up. Getting informed. Low cholesterol, high in fiber - both soluble and non-soluble. That's the order of the day.

No more bacon, sausages and full-fat milk.

One hundred and fifteen LPs in, and not even half way through box two. Just over one percent have been listened to. And it's taken me till Saturday morning. That's over four days. Twenty-five albums a day equates to approximately fifteen hours spent per day on my task.

There is no time to go shopping.

'00116 - Sam Cooke - Night Beat'.

On they go, every one a keeper.

'00128 - The Beatles - With The Beatles'.

It's stereo again. Did he go back to that shop in Tredmouth? I wonder where it was? It could be close to where I sit right now, turning the pedals on my bike at a steady fifteen kilometers per hour.

Did he look for Helen every time he visited?

There are four used record shops in the city now, the internet tells me.

I'd seen bits and bobs on the news about a vinyl revival, and it seems as though it's taken a hold. It's no flash in the pan.

Vinyl revival? Dad never stopped. There was no revival required there.

I'd laugh at him. It was so antiquated, buying old records.

Off he'd go, every Sunday morning to the fairs and car boot sales and jumbles. Come rain, come shine. There was always something on.

He had a shoulder bag he carted with him, It was the correct size for housing albums.

My hands are adept already, to the point I can cue a record up in the dark.

There's no repositioning or adjustment required to find the spindle.

Each time I reach into the box for the next disc, there's a sense of anticipation that goes with the action. I draw it clear and remove the record from the see-through protective outer, before sliding the inner sleeve free.

Propping the vinyl against the box, I gently press the sides of the outer sleeve so it billows. I peer inside.

A tiny pang of sadness accompanies the realisation no letter from my father is contained within.

Maybe next time. Another thirty to forty minutes, and I can repeat the whole process.

It continues in that fashion, up to the point exhaustion hits me, and I have to retire to bed.

It's the next day, Sunday evening, before I get to experience the little euphoric buzz once again.

My smile is already in place, as I come to another Chipmunks LP.

15.

'00155 (play) - TH'.

The LP is housed in a plain white thin paper sleeve, and has a plain white label.

'Ah, you're still with me, Danny son!

How's it going? Are you skipping through the records looking for these notes? I wouldn't blame you if you did.

If not, then it's taken you over a hundred hours to get to this stage, so I appreciate your time and effort.

Everybody is so busy these days. It seems as though nobody has time to sit and listen to anything. Least of all, other people.

Tommy Histon was born Theodore Thomas Marshall Histon in 1932, precise date unknown. Even by him.

His mother told him there was snow on the ground on the day he was born, but in the Appalachians, that could have been any time from early-October through late-April.

It only became relevant when he required a passport to fly to England. He made up a date of February 29th, so that he wouldn't have to think about it too often.

The only birthday he ever knew was in the leap year of 1964.

I know all of this, Danny, because he told me it himself.

That same year, I turned twenty-one. I was a fully-qualified mechanic. Ally Mac - and through him, Baz Baxter - asked me to work for them on weekends and evenings when I was free.

I'd maintain their vehicles, and help out with the occasional driving job.

Great! More money, more records, and more chance to pick from Ally's shelves.

I met a fair few of the music acts of the time, son. Only long enough to shake their hands and have a quick chat about music. But it was a thrill for me, nonetheless.

I think they gave me the Tommy Histon job because nobody who knew anything about him would do it!

That was a baptism of fire, I can tell you.

On a Friday in the spring of that year, I left work early, and drove down to a house in Middlesex where I picked him up.

I should have noticed how nobody seemed sad to see him leave, as the people he'd been staying with shoved him towards me, and ran back into their house, before slamming and locking the door.

He'd only been staying with them for one day, after arrival at the airport.

I loaded his suitcase in the boot of the 1962 Jaguar MK II I'd been assigned for the job, and laid his guitar case on the rear seat.

Hopping in the driver's side, I noticed that he was standing motionless by the passenger door.

Ah, I thought to myself, I'm supposed to open the door for him.

Leaping back out, I scooted round to his side.

"Why is this car back to front?" he asked me in his American drawl.

"Oh, all cars in England have the steering wheel on the other side."

He nodded. "This is earth, correct?"

"What?"

"Planet earth. This is the planet earth?"

"Erm, yes. This is definitely earth."

At that, his hand shot out and grabbed my genitals.

He began to rummage, his eyes averted, and the lids almost closed.

I tried to pull away, but he held me firm, and examined me.

"Two," he announced, releasing me.

"Two what?" I asked, in a state of shock.

"Testicles. You have two."

"Erm, yes. Why? Is that important?"

"Very," he informed me, and let himself into the car.

We set off towards Brakeshire. I was to deliver him to a hotel in Tredmouth, before picking him up the following morning at eight-thirty, and taking him to Ally Mac's place.

How hard could that be?

"The testicle thing..." I ventured, as I drove north.

"Had to check. My apologies for that."

"Why?"

"To make sure you ain't one of them," he said, and pointed upwards.

"Them?"

"Aliens. They only have one. It's how you tell 'em from us."

"Right."

"It's on account of their momma's only having one ovary."

"Okay."

"Shrind el pas ng-ng-ng tormu belzee," he said, as though it were a continuation of the conversation.

I must have looked at him like he was completely bonkers. Which he was.

"You don't understand that?" he enquired.

"Erm, no." I chuckled.

"If you did, I'd slay you here and now."

"Right."

"If you had one testicle, and understood that, you'd be dead in a fuckin' heartbeat."

"Then I'm glad I don't."

"What's your name?"

"Bill."

"I'm Tommy."

"I know."

"How do you know?" he snapped, scowling at me.

"Because I'm employed to drive you to your hotel. And it helps if I know who I'm picking up."

"Okay," he accepted, and somewhat relaxed.

We sat in silence for half an hour. It was intimidating, that total silence.

It began to rain. He opened the window and rested his arm outside.

After a few minutes, he flung his arm back in and spattered me with water.

I was startled, and swore, as he peered closely at my face in the light from the oncoming traffic.

"You're all good, Bill. They don't like water. Truth is, I had to be sure. Now, I could feel that your testicles were intact and connected, but they have ways of adding a fake one. So, I couldn't rely on that alone now, could I?"

"No. I suppose not."

"And you could have been acting about not understanding the language, right?"

"I suppose."

"You know how I know that lingo?"

"No," I told him, because I didn't have a clue.

"My poppa taught me. And his poppa taught him. And so on. Right back to god himself, or some other asshole, teaching someone who passed it on via word of mouth. It ain't writ down, I can tell you that."

"Okay."

"You know how you can tell them aliens?"

"Through the testicles?"

"No. Well, yes. But, no. They can't tell the future. They only know the past."

"Erm, I think you'll find that..."

"They study us, and they know all that has gone before. But they have no clue what will happen even a second from now."

"Right."

"See, now, I know that you will have to hit them brakes hard, and slow this car in twenty-four seconds from now."

"Right."

We waited, the pair of us, the wiper blade whipping water from the screen. I couldn't help but count those seconds in my head, Danny. I was determined not to brake, no matter what.

It occurred to me that he would reach over and grab the steering wheel, or something, so I was on my guard.

As I approached my count, a car slid on the wet surface ahead, veering into our side of the road.

I hit the brakes.

And Tommy Histon laughed for two minutes solid.

"How did you know?" I asked him eventually.

"They took me, and they probed my brain, Bill. They tried to tap into that power of mine, because it was the one thing they didn't have that we do. They wanted to learn from me how to do it."

"And did they?" I couldn't believe I was asking him that in all seriousness.

"Oh, no, Billy boy. I never let them see."

"How did you get that scar on your face?"

It ran from the corner of his right eye down to the tip of his chin in a slight curve.

"Something and nothing. I checked out a man I suspected of being an alien. It was outside a bar in some shitty little one-horse town in Vermont. Anyways, he didn't take kindly to my examination, so he cut me with a knife he carried."

"Sorry to hear that."

"Oh, don't be. Real lucky for me, he cut me in the exact same location as the aliens had opened me up, so it made no difference to my appearance."

Danny, he was insane. But he was also a genius, musically speaking.

And I got pretty fond of him, over the course of a couple of days.

To this day, I've wondered how he knew I'd have to hit the brakes on exactly twenty-four seconds. I've never been able to explain it.

We finally arrived back in Brakeshire. It was late, and he refused to stay at the hotel that had been booked for him. Apparently, it was the wrong colour and shape.

He suggested I drop him at an all-night bar, and he'd sort himself out.

This was 1964, and there were no all-night bars in Tredmouth. It was close to eleven, and the rain was still lashing down.

I was tired, Danny. I'd worked all day since six, and driven for hours. All I wanted, was to sit down and have a beer before hitting the hay.

"Look, you can kip at mine," I offered, mainly as a way of achieving that end.

He could have my bed, and I'd take the sofa.

No answer came. His eyes stared at me unblinkingly, his head slightly over to one side as we drove through the city centre.

"Say that again," he growled.

"You can kip at mine," I repeated.

In the blink of an eye, a knife point was pressing into my ear. Apparently, that was the only way to kill an alien.

"How do you know that word?" he asked, his voice slow and low.

"What word?"

"Kip."

"It's... It's a word. An English word."

"No it fuckin' ain't."

"It is!" I insisted. I was starting to get a bit worried.

"Only one way you could know that word. You fooled me with the testicle."

"No! Look, I'll stop and ask someone. It's an English word that you might not know in America."

I went to pull over alongside a man walking home.

"Not him," Tommy hissed, "he could be one of yours. Him over there. We'll ask him," he said, pointing at a man striding towards us.

The hand holding the knife dropped down out of sight, and he wound down the window on his side.

"Hey buddy," he called out, "who's going to win the Grand National tomorrow?"

"Team Spirit, if I'm lucky," the man smiled back.

"Ah, you can see the future. That's good. Real good. Now, you know the word kip?"

"Kip?"

"Yeah, kip. You know that word, buddy?"

"Yes, it means sleep. And that's what I'm going to do right now."

As the man walked on, Tommy called after him, "you going to the Grand National?"

"Not me, no."

"Good," said Tommy, "I'm glad about that. They'll be watching from the sky. Wouldn't want you getting hurt by any fire falling from above."

We drove away, Tommy Histon happy that I was human, and delighted to be able to kip over at my place.

En route, I asked him, "so, what does kip mean in alien language?"

"Potassium permanganate," he answered without pause, and lit a cigarette.

"Right," seemed like the only suitable reply.

We sat up half of the night playing music, drinking beer and chatting. He picked on his guitar as we did.

All of it was peppered with his paranoid delusions, Danny, but I could see and hear the creative brilliance in him.

I dropped him at Ally Mac's the next morning as agreed, and picked him up in the evening. He spent another night on my sofa (he refused to take my bed).

On the Sunday lunchtime, I drove him over to a remote house near Norton Bassett. It was fitted out with a recording studio, and everything he could need.

He seemed happy to stay there. It was the right shape and colour.

Ally and Baz had started a record label called Chemisette, and Tommy Histon was to record the first release for it.

They'd flown him over and picked up all of the expenses.

Histon had enjoyed some cult success in the fifties, a few years after recording and releasing what many believe to be one of, if not the first rock'n'roll, or rockabilly LP in 1949. He was sixteen when he recorded it.

His next two albums in '53 and '54 were folk-rock records before folk-rock had been labelled as such.

As he said to me that night in my flat, "because I can see the future further than any other asshole, I'm always destined to be ahead of my time, Bill. And that ain't good, to be too far ahead of the pack. No matter what I do, the world just ain't ready for Tommy Histon."

And he was right. I picked up those albums on re-issue many years later, and they're on these shelves. They sound like something from another time, when you put them in context. They come from a decade before they should have emerged. And had they been released ten years after they were recorded, I think they may have been massive hits.

They weren't, though, so they flopped and were quickly deleted. But a cult following grew up around them, added to by the myth and truth surrounding the mad-genius of the man himself. His cult status has only grown over the years.

A few weeks after I dropped him at the house over by Norton Bassett, I was awoken one night by a rhythmic rapping on the door.

I got up, went down, and opened up to see Tommy Histon standing on the step. He had a crash-helmet on his head, that appeared to be wrapped in tinfoil. I invited him in, but he declined the invitation.

In his hand was his guitar case. It, too, was wrapped in tinfoil.

"Can't stay. Got to run, Bill. They found me, the sons of bitches," he informed me, his index finger pointing upwards.

"Just come in, Tommy. We'll talk about it." I could see that he was in a bad way mentally. His eyes were staringly mad and bloodshot, and there was sweat coating his face.

"No can do, Bill. They can't trace me with this on," he said, tapping his helmet, "but I need to draw them fuckers away from you, buddy. You still have things to do in this world."

"Do I?"

"Oh, yeah, boy. Me? I'm all used up. I have nothing more to offer, Bill. Well, let them fuckers come for me now. I'm ready," he said, and pulled up his shirt to show that he had a pistol tucked down his waistband.

"Shit, Tommy," I said. I'd never seen a real gun before. "We can sort it out, whatever it is," I urged him.

"I need a promise from you, Bill," he said, letting his shirt flop back down, and taking my hand in his.

His irises found my pupils, and I noticed the little tremor in them.

"What do you need, Tommy?"

"I need you to take this," he said, and squatted to open his guitar case.

He held out a twelve inch package that I knew was a record. I went to take it, but he held firm and didn't release his grip.

"That promise I mentioned," he said.

"What do you need me to do?"

"I require you to take these two copies of my record. One is for you to play, but only ever when you're alone. The other is the master - that should never be played by you. That is for someone else, who will collect it from you. When the time's right, this record will be taken by the right person, and you have to let them have it. Will you promise me, Bill?"

"I promise."

"You are the custodian, understand?"

"Yes."

"You're a good man, Bill Goods. Thank you for everything."

He walked off into the night.

For nearly fifty years I kept my promise, Danny. And now I'm dying, and this record will go to you. The second copy has never been played. The first has only ever been heard by me.

I have no idea what happens next, or if anything of what he said was true or of any consequence. I have no clue.

Two weeks later, I was called over to Ally Mac's. Baz Baxter was present. I remember being happy as I drove over towards Millby on that bright morning, and the prospect of spending more time with Tommy.

They told me that Tommy Histon's guitar case had been found on a beach in Anglesey. It was empty. The only other thing at the scene was a foil covered crash helmet.

His body washed up a day later.

It looked as though he'd walked out on the rocks that jutted out, and stabbed himself through his ear before slipping into the sea.

Prior to his disappearance, he'd destroyed all of the test-pressing copies of his completed album, as well as the master tapes, pressing plates and lacquers. There was nothing left of it.

All they had to show for their expense, was a tape of acoustic demo songs that he laid down prior to recording them properly.

The album was titled 'Kimono For Kip'.

"Did you see him in the last two weeks, Bill?" Baz Baxter asked me.

"No," I replied, because I hadn't. It had been a little longer than that since he'd knocked my door.

"And he didn't give you anything?"

"Sure. He gave me an inspection," I said, and they chuckled.

That's why I always kept my records in the order that I got them, Danny. So it would be more difficult for anybody to find. There was no H section to go to, and Tommy Histon would never be conveniently located somewhere between Françoise Hardy and Buddy Holly.

Later on, I thought about reordering things, but it always seemed like too much of an undertaking by then, as my collection had grown.

It was also why I stashed both copies inside Chipmunks sleeves. It seemed oddly apt.

Nobody ever came to collect the record.

I don't know what you're supposed to do with it, son. I suppose it's, ultimately, up to you now.

You'll do what's right and what's best. I trust you.

Well, that was a long old tale.

I'm tired now.

I get so tired lately.

Till next time.

Love, Dad.

PS - I put half a quid on that horse at eighteen to one, and it came in!'

16.

I have a degree in chemistry. The interest came from a chemistry set I was given as a birthday gift by Ally Mac when I was ten years old.

Of course, I never did anything with my degree. It was easier to get a job in marketing. When I say marketing, I mean I work on a local paper selling classified advertising space.

Sometimes, I get to write a small article on an insignificant event that took place in Tredmouth which nobody cares about.

I wouldn't call my job fulfilling.

In fact, it's barely a job. Most of it is now done on-line. The old print format is dead.

Sure enough, two copies of the album exist in the box, numbered '00155 (play) - TH' and '00156 (keep) - TH'.

Beyond those labels, my father's letter is the only indicator of the true contents. Both are housed in Chipmunks sleeves.

Thanks to my degree, and many hours spent learning chemical formulae, I know that potassium permanganate is $KMnO4$.

Kimono For.

Kip.

Alien speak for potassium permanganate, according to a story told by my old man.

He wasn't so old, though.

He used to tell his tales, but I didn't really listen.

Any mention of having to collect someone, MIddlesex, or staying in a hotel, would invariably prompt him to say, "I remember picking up Tommy Histon from this house in Middlesex, and taking him to a hotel."

How I wish I'd listened.

As the LP plays, I look Tommy Histon up on-line.

Wow!

There's loads on him, from all over the world, and it ties in to all that dad wrote about.

Original copies of his three albums, those that saw the light of day, are hugely coveted. They sold so few back when they were released, that people will pay a small fortune to own them now.

Sadly, dad only has those on much later reissues, as he revealed in his letter.

The acoustic demo versions he mentioned have been released on CD and vinyl many times over the intervening years, and are readily available for not much money.

Chat and articles I unearth on the internet speculate about the survival of the finished and unreleased fourth album. But nobody is sure of its existence.

And, apparently, I'm sat on an exercise bike listening to it.

I could be the second person to hear this record in fifty-five years.

It's weirdly beautiful, and completely out of sync with every record I've listened to up to this point.

However, even my limited knowledge of music is sufficient to tell me that, come the late-sixties and early-seventies, this would fit right in.

I find an old interview with the recording engineer at the sessions in Norton Bassett, who describes the record as being "acid-folk and space-rock long before such things had been invented."

Ha! People actually go to the house that dad dropped Tommy at, as part of some sort of pilgrimage. From there, they head off to Anglesey, to visit the headland and rocky outcrop where he died.

My father knew this man. He slept on his sofa.

In a flash, it dawns on me that my dad was really fucking cool.

I read that the album title, 'Kimono For Kip', is believed to have been inspired by a visit to Ally McIntyre's house just prior to recording. That must have been when my dad dropped him there on the Saturday!

The article states, "McIntyre, a cross-dresser of some renown, opened the door to Histon dressed in a silk kimono that he allegedly slept in. Hence, 'Kimono For Kip'. Note: this may also explain the purple silk referred to in the lyrics."

Page follows page on Tommy Histon, as the engineer talks about him "getting sounds out of instruments and other objects he'd find lying around, that were like nothing ever heard before."

A comparison is made to Joe Meek, and I recall the 'Telstar' album I played a couple of days ago. Yes, I can hear the similarity in terms of sound. But this Histon LP is far more beautiful than that.

His voice is high and breathy, not unlike Gene Vincent. The melodies are unbelievably catchy and familiar, but, at the same time, unique. They're the type of tunes you feel sure you must have heard before.

The lyrics are half-nonsensical, dipping in and out of refrains you can somewhat decrypt, and morphing into the alien language that dad wrote down. Or something very much like it, at least.

There's much on-line speculation about that, as people attempt to extract the words from those ropey demos, and fathom what on earth (or not of this earth) Tommy was singing about.

They play the record backwards, looking for hidden messages!

It's as I'm checking the 1964 Grand National result, that a word on the record corresponds with a word I'm reading.

Supersweet.

It finished twelfth.

Dismounting the bike, I restart the album, the runners in the National open in front of me.

And as I listen, I pick them out - Peacetown (3rd) is the location being sought, and the Eternal (4th) Claymore (13th), clad in Purple Silk (2nd), sheltering in Pappageno's Cottage (10th), as the machine Flying Wild (non-finisher) falls from the sky in flames.

Other non-finishers arrest my ears - Border Flight and Lizawake, woken by the din of destruction, as the Groomsman, Laffy, pulls her clear of the carnage, through the Dancing Rain, and away to John O'Groats (11th), where she learns he is Beau of Normandy, L'Empereur of Red Thorn, as the Sea Knight (15th) watches on and silently calls all to his water, where they can be safe from the flames, and cleansed of the demons that occupy their minds.

The whole album is a concept, twisting those horse names around an apocalyptic invasion of fiery Crobegs (9th).

And nobody, it appears, has ever worked out where all of the references came from. Until now.

Alien words pepper every song - a strange undecipherable language that seems to me to have been inserted because it sounded right, and matched the song. In fact, it sounds more like an instrument than lyrics, thanks to Tommy's ethereal delivery.

An article points out that The Cocteau Twins would use unrecognisable lyrics two decades later.

I'm left with no doubt that I'm listening to something utterly unique, and quite remarkable.

A foot note draws my attention on the Grand National - the further reading section. It tells of a plane crash near the course before the race began. Five people were killed.

A line in the final song seems to make reference to it, as Nancy took Laurie to Spain. Joan Werner Laurie and Nancy Spain were two of the victims.

I seem to have pieced it all together, the much-speculated-on meaning behind the songs. Remove my knowledge of the Grand National, and I suppose it would be hard to make the connection. Histon made just enough subtle changes to the names so as to throw people off the scent.

He skewed it all with his pronunciations and slight shifts, from Beau Normand to Beau of Norman D, which made it sound like Beau Normandy.

I don't even think that dad knew what it was all about.

Oh, I wish he was alive.

If he was here, I could show him all I've discovered. He'd be tickled pink, I bet.

If only I'd given the man some time to tell me his stories. Had I done that, I might have connected the dots while he was still around to hear me.

There was a runner called Time in that 1964 Grand National. It didn't go the distance. It fell short.

Another was called Reprieved. It was an outsider.

But it pulled up and refused to negotiate one of the obstacles in its path.

I've spent enough time on this record. It's time to move on.

I bend to remove it from the platter. As I do, the light catches the run-off groove.

Lifting it, I tilt it so the scant sunlight catches the smooth dark strip before the white label.

There's an etched number, 'CH-770001', which I think relates to the intended label and release number, this being the planned debut on Chemisette Records.

Next to that are other hand-etched characters.

Scratchy, but clear, they read '2B, 4D, postP'.

'To Bill, for Danny, after Paula' is how I interpret them.

17.

Everything sounds a little tame and dated for a while after the Tommy Histon album.

It isn't, but it takes some time for my ears and brain to adjust.

I can see and hear, as 1964 progressed, that the music dad was buying became more familiar. The Kinks and The Animals, for example. Many of the tracks on the records are known to me.

That familiarity could have come through dad playing them, but I think not. They're the classics you hear on the radio, or on television shows, or even in the pub.

Enter any artist into a device, and allow it free rein to play other music that might appeal, and it'll get to the Bob Dylan, Beach Boys and Beatles music of 1964.

It's all great, but I find myself hungry for something more challenging.

Besides which, I should probably be searching the house for an intruder. After all, somebody must have broken in. How else did the bike come to have over one hundred kilometers showing on the computer?

It's Sunday night. Late. Perhaps even Monday morning, strictly speaking. A week ago, I fell down the stairs, and spent the night in hospital.

It was nice of Lisa to ring and see how I am.

But, then, why should she?

I wasn't willing to give her what she wanted. So, she went and found it with someone else. That's her priority now, the family she always craved.

Family was never very important to me. Rather, I believed that I didn't need it in my life.

After dad died, I was angry. I felt slighted.

I will concede, I'm getting a lot more out of these records, personally speaking, than I ever believed I would. It's true to say of both the music itself, and the messages tucked inside the sleeves.

And the cumulative financial value is growing all the time.

However, it hardly compares to a share of the house, the furnishings within, and the business that went to Trevor.

Granted, my brother worked with dad from leaving school, and took on the business after he was forced to take a step back. But for me to get nothing from it was a kick in the teeth.

Similarly, I moved away when the others remained close, and my sisters popped round and looked out for him as his health declined. But, again, to get nothing was a slap in the face to go along with the teeth kicking.

We weren't on great money, despite the impression that I may have given to the contrary. I'd laud it over my small-town family - those closed-minded relatives of mine. Not one of them ever lived more than five miles from where they were born.

I didn't want to be like that. I wanted to see places, and live in a city that had more to offer than Palmerton bloody Chase.

Yet, even now, I'm barely making ends meet. In fact, I haven't been making ends meet since Lisa left, and took her income with her.

Over the past year, I've amassed an unhealthy overdraft and a high-interest loan, both of which are crippling me.

But the debts were there long before Lisa left. We were living beyond our means, and reliant on credit.

How different would things have been had I inherited my fair share?

And, to my shame, I had been somewhat waiting for dad to die, so that I could bail myself out.

He was irrecoverably ill, so his demise was an inevitability. I presumed a quarter share of the house, and planned accordingly.

And then they shafted me.

I accused my sisters of manipulating dad to change his Will. With hindsight, I don't believe they maliciously did that, and I feel guilty for the things I charged them with.

My big mouth cost me my family.

All of that said, I don't think I would have done what they did. It was unjust, and I would have made some conciliatory offer. I would have done the right thing.

They took the money and ran.

Actually, they didn't run. They remained where they'd always been, and would always be. Palmerton Chase, that safe little village-town, where everybody knows everybody and their business.

How come, therefore, I ended up being the narrow-minded one?

Because dad never was. He was into everything, judging by his record collection.

18.

1964 continues, and moves into and through 1965: Simon And Garfunkel - Wednesday Morning, 3AM. Yardbirds - Five Live Yardbirds. John Barry - Goldfinger. Manfred Mann - The Five Faces Of Manfred Mann. The Hollies - In The Hollies Style. Gerry Mulligan - Butterfly With Hiccups. The Who - My Generation. The Pretty Things - self-titled.

It goes on. Sam Cooke is still present, The Impressions, Motown albums begin to appear.

Methodically, I continue to play every record. A-side first. Then flip it over for the B-side.

Dad always put them away with the A-side facing the front of the sleeve, I notice. It makes me grin, that little quirk of his.

Before I know it, it's Tuesday night. It's late-1965 in my dad's world. It's taken me nearly three hundred kilometers to reach it.

It's not that far.

The Byrds, Junior Wells, Marianne Faithful, Art Blakey.

'00222 - Davy Graham - Folk, Blues And Beyond'.

'00223 - Jackson C Frank - self-titled'.

'00224 - The Beatles - Rubber Soul'.

'Hello Danny.

Late-1965 was the time I fell hopelessly in love.

I seriously fell in love with music, as I found my niche. It was much like trying on an off-the-peg suit that fitted perfectly.

Davy Graham and Jackson C Frank were that clothing made to measure.

Up to this point, I was smitten with music. I shan't deny that. But these albums tipped me over to another level.

In my opinion, both are utterly brilliant.

Davy Graham was interpreting other people's songs in the main, many of which I was already familiar with. As will you be, if you played these albums in order...

Jackson C Frank wrote his own. And what songs they are!

These two albums changed me, son. They altered the way that I thought and listened. They made me more reflective.

Jazz and soul would chill me out, and relax me after a hard day's graft. Rock music would energise me. Other music might make me smile or make me sad.

But these albums, along with Tommy Histon's, were the real me. They are where my heart lies. Others would come later that fit the mould, but this was the real beginning.

All of that said, it is The Beatles 'Rubber Soul' that soundtracks the next chapter in my life.

Time and place, Danny. Never discount the importance of that. Even a bad record can hold allure because of the memories it holds in its grooves.

Not that 'Rubber Soul' is a bad record. Far from it.

Besides, it isn't actually mine. But it sits here in my collection, because it came to me at that time.

I was twenty-two, and for the first time in my life, I lived with a woman.

I loved her, Danny. And the record was hers.

Her name was Madeleine.

She came up by train from London to work for Baz Baxter. So, through Ally Mac, he had me meet her at the station in Tredmouth. She was a model, and she looked just as you'd expect a model in 1965 London to look.

She wanted to design clothes, so Baxter brought her on-board to add glamour to his Tredmouth clubs. And to come up with a range of designs, in line with London trends, to sell to a hungry public through a shop he owned called 'It's

Tred Dad!'. That was a none-too-subtle play on a film from a few years before, titled 'It's Trad Dad!'.

Well, I was Jack The Lad as I escorted Miss Madeleine Michey along the platform that day, I can tell you. All eyes were on us, as I cockily ordered a porter to bring her cases to the car.

A photographer from the Tredmouth Echo was in attendance, tipped off by Baz to get a bit of free publicity. I was in a picture that appeared a couple of weeks before Christmas. Well, part of me is, at least, as I walked beside her.

It's the same newspaper you produce each week, Danny. That's always made me very proud of you, the knowledge that I barely made a grainy image appearing on page nine, and you pull the thing together every seven days!

I slipped the porter a couple of bob for being a good chap, and assisted Madeleine into the car.

God, those legs, son! They went on for ever, before disappearing into a pair of black boots. I don't know the correct terms, but she wore a bright red sort of tunic dress that barely covered her privates, and beneath it a very tight, thin, long-sleeved, black sweater.

Now, this was Brakeshire in December, and I could have hung my coat and hat on her nipples!

In the car, she sat shivering so badly, that I pulled over after a mile and gave her my long wool coat to wear.

She didn't thank me. She nodded her appreciation, though. She later told me that she was too cold to speak, as her teeth were chattering.

Baz had made her wear something revealing for the press.

Her hair was jet-black and had a sheen that I'd never seen on any girl in Brakeshire. Her skin was pale like milk, and her brown eyes made-up with dark liner that made them appear huge and sad.

Seeing how I was assigned to running her around, we got to chat a bit, and spend some time together. We slowly got to know one another over a couple of months.

Anyway, come the February of 1966, I drove her over to some town or other in Northamptonshire, to look at and collect fabric.

I'd left the garage I'd served my time in by then, and was working full-time for Ally and Baz, as I looked for premises in which to open my own business.

The weather came on in a blizzard as we headed back to Brakeshire that day, and worsened as I neared the county. At one point, I thought we weren't going to make it. We slid a quarter of a mile backwards negotiating the high ground on the east border, the ice was so bad.

Make it we did, and I gingerly dropped down into Palmerton Chase. There was no way either of us wanted to risk the forty mile run to Tredmouth, so Madeleine stayed at mine.

She hated living alone in a room above 'It's Tred Dad!' so remained at mine after that night.

At first, I took the sofa and she had my bed.

Now, whether it was lack of inhibition, or because she felt secure around me, I had no idea. She was very cool, and wasn't one for showing her feelings or revealing her thoughts. But she would, from the first day, parade around my flat in just her underwear. And sometimes, not even that.

I reasoned she was so used to undressing and dressing in her profession, that it was of no consequence to her. Nakedness didn't seem to bother her in the slightest.

I never imagined for one second that she fancied me.

Well, I'd try to be gentlemanly, and avert my eyes. But I didn't try too hard!

The problem with my flat was the bath water. The boiler was old and knackered, and you could never get enough to fill the tub before it went cold. I'd fill every pan I owned, and heat water on the stove to eke out enough to make it bearable.

It took ages, and with two of us using it, it wasn't far off a full-time job managing things.

About two weeks after she moved in, I'd had a bad day fixing one of Baz's vans. I was covered in oil and grime, and aching from head to toe, working out in the cold to get the thing running.

On arrival home, I could hear Madeleine filling a bath, the pans all bubbling away on the stovetop.

I smiled and shook my head, and decided to make do with a wash in the sink. I was all in, son, and was only thinking of a beer or two with an album or two, before getting my head down.

Therein lay another problem. Whilst the rent money was handy, as I saved for my deposit on the garage premises, I could never go to bed on the sofa until she retired to the bedroom for the evening.

Take a look at the cover of the Jackson C Frank LP, Danny. That's my oily thumb print from the night I describe. I intended to clean it off after a refreshing beer.

Madeleine heard the music and came through, stark naked. She took one look at me, noticed the appalling state I was in - I looked like I'd come home from the pit after an accident - and suggested I take the bath water.

I protested, and reassured her that I was fine, that I was too tired anyway, and wanted nothing more than to sit and unwind.

She took my oily hand, Dan, and led me to the bathroom. She honestly was the most perfect physical specimen of a woman I'd ever seen. And there she was, undressing me out of my filthy overalls.

When I was as naked as her, she helped me step into the tub. I sank down, self-consciously letting the bubbles cover my bits and bobs.

She ferried the pans of water in, and swished the warmth all around me with her hands, before lathering up the soap and washing me all over. And I mean all over!

It transpired that she'd refilled the pans and kettle, so more warm water was fetched by her. And then she stepped into the tub with me, sank down between my legs, and washed herself in the oil-slicked water I'd spoiled.

That night, and for the next six months, we lived like a married couple.

I never slept on the sofa again, and I never got round to cleaning the thumb print off the cover of the Jackson C Frank album.

By the time I reencountered it, I decided to leave it as a reminder. And there it's been for nigh on fifty years.

One thing I will tell you, is that I missed half of England's World Cup triumph that summer. We had no television at home, and had planned to go and watch it round at my parents' place.

I left work a bit early. It was quiet anyway, as everyone was glued to their televisions. Madeleine would run me a bath, as we'd discussed, so I rushed through the door tugging my overalls off as I went.

By the time I got to the kitchen, off the back of which was the bathroom, I was stark naked.

In I flew, and there's my Aunt Bet stood at the sink, the kettle in her hand, and no sign of Maddie.

I grabbed a tea-towel from the counter, and covered up as best I could.

"Milk and sugar, Billy?" she asked, as though it was the most normal everyday occurrence.

"Please," said I, "where's Madeleine?"

"She's gone over to try and help your father get the television working. The aerial fell off the roof. I said I'd come here and run your bath. Now, get your skates on, or we'll miss kick-off!"

She held my tea out to me.

I took it in one hand, maintained a grip on the tea-towel with my other, and sidled out the back as best I could.

Dear Aunt Bet had run my bath for me.

I did love that woman, Dan, almost as much as I loved my mum.

Kick-off was less than half an hour away!

I emerged after a few minutes, a bath towel wrapped around me, and got dressed as quickly as I could.

As we went to leave, Aunt Bet said, "any chance I could have my hat back, Billy love?"

It took me a few seconds to work out that I'd snatched up her floppy red and white striped sun-hat and not a tea-towel.

Fetching it from the bathroom, I handed it to her.

She plopped it on her head, and never said anything more about it.

By the time I got over to mum and dad's, fixed the aerial, and had everything working, it was ten minutes into the second half.

And, it seemed, every time I saw Aunt Bet for about two years after that day, she'd be wearing the bloody hat. Along with a cheeky smile on her face.

"My lucky hat!" she'd tease me, "it's seen some sights, you know?"

Ha! I've never told a soul that story, son.

I didn't even remember it until I got to the summer of 1966. I wonder what other tales I'll be reminded of.

Moreover, I wonder how many I've forgotten.

For now, though, my oxygen tank is getting low. That's not a metaphor. It really is. Your sisters should be coming soon to change it, and to check on me.

They're angels to me, Danny. They bring food round every day, and wash me as I sit on a stool in the shower. It's wrong that they have to do that, but they insist they don't mind.

As Beth said last week, "but you bathed us when we were little, so this is us returning the service!"

I laughed at that, but laughing leaves me short of air, son. They get worried, Beth and Yvonne, when that happens. So I try not to laugh too much with them.

These letters to you, though. I've had some laughs writing those. I hope you have, too.

I can hear the key in the door. I'd best sign off for now.

See you, pal.

Love, Dad.'

19.

It takes an effort to stop myself searching for Madeleine Michey on the web.

What will it reveal? Her image, perhaps. The end of her life. That's how it goes on the internet. Date of birth and date of death are the first things you see. Cut to the chase, and discover the ending in the first chapter.

It'll render the story that took her there irrelevant. I'd rather my dad tell it. Besides, only her time with my father holds any allure for me. Without that, she's of no import.

I'm of the generation used to having data at its fingertips. I can know anything in seconds, simply by tapping it into my phone.

I switch it off.

Music's the same. It must be twenty years since I last listened to an album in its entirety. Prior to the past ten days, at least.

Devices mean that I can skip straight to the 'hit', or upload a compilation of the 'hits'. There's no context, therefore. There's less art as a result.

Do albums even matter in modern music? Probably not. It's all about the two tracks on it that will generate revenue through downloads and airplay. The rest is something of an irrelevance. Literally, filler.

Dad would pontificate about it any chance he got. But I never listened. I didn't care.

Until now.

Another thing that strikes me, is my dad's intelligence. I never even knew he could write, beyond a greeting card or a shopping list.

For all the years we shared a life on this planet, I only ever saw him as a car mechanic. That was all he'd ever done, since he left school with no real qualifications.

My brother, Trev, followed suit.

As a result, I considered myself to be superior.

Ultimately, his life, even to 1966, was infinitely more interesting than mine.

I am inferior.

I'd secretly, and sometimes openly, sneer at him for his working-class, blue-collar job, and his habit of visiting car boot and jumble sales. I'd shake my head at his daft room full of records. What a waste of space and effort. Not to mention time and money.

He'd ask me if I fancied going over to some town or other, for a record fair. And I'd shake my head and pull a face to imply what a ridiculous waste of life it would be.

Until, one day, he stopped asking.

And I was relieved. He could do his thing, and I'd do mine.

But what the fuck did I do?

My superior life? It's stretched out on the sofa, prior to Lisa taking it, watching television or playing a game, not one second of which is of any consequence to anything.

I exaggerated my role in the world, and played up all of my paltry achievements.

Oh, to listen to me, I ran the fucking local paper. Without me, it would cease to be. The world would very possibly end, were I not to get out of bed, don my cheap suit and threadbare white-collar shirt, and go to the office.

People like my dad couldn't imagine the level of responsibility involved in what I did. I might not be getting covered in oil and fitting new exhausts, but the taxing of my brain was far more exhausting.

What a load of bollocks.

My father owned the business. It was the Goods name above the door and on the stationery. He employed my brother. He owned the house that he left to my sisters.

My job is insignificant. All I have to show for my endeavours, is this two-bed rented terraced house in a crap part of town.

And I'm nearly fucking forty, and only just working this out.

I have no relationship. I have no friends. Not really. They exist virtually, these acquaintances I've never met. They are virtually worthless.

Had I broken my neck, when I fell down the stairs, how long would I have lain there before anybody noticed? Would it have been the smell of my rotting flesh that would have first alerted anyone?

And even that would have only come about because of the stench being an inconvenience to my neighbours.

I imagine the pungence of decomposing flesh might have a derogatory effect on property prices, after all.

Pedals turn as I think my thoughts.

As do the records.

Love, Yardbirds, Nancy Sinatra, Martin Carthy, The Monkees and The Sonics help take me through the year of 1966.

I find myself wondering what the weather was like, of all things. And how the world looked and smelled.

Images of my young dad and Madeleine Michey, with her short black shining hair, a miniskirt and boots, pepper my mind's eye, as they stroll through Palmerton Chase hand in hand.

Did they ramble northward following the Brake canal, before taking the grass path out over the fields and ascending the Brake Hills to the east?

Did they have sex up there in some private little spot?

Even though it was before my mum entered his life, I find it a little upsetting to think of him with another woman.

How silly.

None of the records I play through 1966 contain communication from my dad. Is it because there was nothing to tell, or because he doesn't want to tell me?

He said he would be honest.

Ah, it's none of my business. It was a life before I was ever a thought, let alone conceived. The two people from which I am constituted hadn't even met.

My brother, Trevor, wouldn't appear for another three years. I was fourteen away from making a presence on this earth.

Hours and days pass by, and on I pedal, my legs, ears and brain getting a good work out.

I'm heading somewhere, but I don't know where. It's a journey that takes me to places far from any I've ever visited before. And all without moving.

But I know that I am moved.

20.

'00276 - Tim Hardin - Tim Hardin I'.

'Hello again, Danny.

What time of day is it there, as you read this? It's the evening here, and I'm waiting for the day to close so I can go to bed.

If I head off too early, I wake too early, and the mornings are the loneliest. That waking alone, and getting out of bed, before shuffling through to the kitchen to put the kettle on is the worst time.

It's because I only prepare a single cup, and fill the kettle just enough for one.

And that's the instant at which it's brought home to me that Paula isn't with me, and my children have lives of their own.

I miss you all.

I hope you aren't missing me at all, and are living a full and happy life. I'm sure you are.

You were always the one I didn't have to worry about.

Too much of your mum was present in you, and because of it, I always knew you'd be okay.

You both possess an independence that frees you. My nature is very much 'better the devil you know'. I have a loyalty that restricts me, I suppose. You don't have that. Nor did Paula. You both had an ability to walk away and begin again.

You know your own minds.

I am a dog. You two are cats.

It was always a comfort to me, knowing that about Paula. I never had any doubt that she was with me because she wanted to be.

Had she not, she'd have left.

The other three of my children, I fear, always had a little too many of my genes in their mix. And because I know my own shortcomings, I recognise theirs all too well.

Don't get me wrong, they're wonderful - all four of you are.

I didn't achieve much in life, I suppose, in the great scheme of things. And what I did achieve, I did for her. And, later, for you kids.

I worked hard, Danny, but I aimed small. I did that so, if and when it went wrong, I wouldn't have far to fall.

But back to the music!

This album is a bittersweet one for me.

For weeks on end, in the late-Summer of 1966, it was all I listened to.

Thereafter, for a year and a half, I couldn't bear to listen to it.

I came home from work with it in my hand, having waited for it since its release in, I think, the July of that year. For reasons since lost to me, I had trouble getting hold of a copy.

More likely, seeing how it was the summer I opened the garage, is I simply hadn't had time to collect it.

I do remember I read a review of it in one of the music papers of the time, and enough reference points were present to stoke my interest.

The music press and word of mouth were the only ways of getting information on new releases at the time. It was either that, or discover it in a shop. Quite often, I'd buy a record just because the artwork looked cool.

This was more of a planned purchase.

It has haunted me ever since, this album. From 'Don't Make Promises', through 'It'll Never Happen Again', it is the album above all others that can reduce me to tears.

It's strange, isn't it? Life, I mean. I got back home that day - a Saturday, meaning I had the Sunday off - and I remember vividly a sense of utter contentment. I was so, so happy.

I had my latest record in hand, and business was great. Ally Mac and Baz Baxter had come through with their contracts for service, and I knew I'd be okay - more than okay - for the next few years.

My girlfriend was a stunningly beautiful model, and I was the envy of every man in Palmerton Chase, not to mention further afield!

I was proud of all I'd achieved by the ripe old age of twenty-three.

Watch out for pride, Danny. Promise me that, son?

And never get too comfortable, for that's when life tends to deal you a bad hand. It knows. Get too smug and cocky, and something will come along to rip it all to shreds.

'Homeward Bound', I was, and I sang it in the car at the top of my voice - where my music's playing and my love lies waiting.

We'd have a bath together, and shift all of the week from me. The September weather was forecast to be perfect, and we'd planned to drive out to the countryside on Sunday.

Madeleine left a note. One line.

She wanted more from life, Danny. She desired something that I was a million miles from.

It was a life that didn't interest me. I prefer being a bigger sprat in a small pool.

That said, had she asked me to go with her, I believe I would have done. For her, I'd have walked away from all I knew.

My natural risk averseness wouldn't have come into play.

There was no address or phone number on the note. There was no trail to follow. I presumed she'd gone back to London.

Oh, but she broke my heart, son.

Tim Hardin seemed to know exactly how I felt.

And when I got to 'How Can We Hang On To A Dream?', I was a blubbering wreck.

Even now, sitting here listening to it as I write this note to you, the tears burn my eyes and painfully clamp my throat.

Forty-six years on, and it still gets me.

She's walking away. She's saying we're through.

How can we hang on to a dream?

We can't, Danny. Not always. And sometimes, you have to let people go.

I'm going to go for now. I'm sad, and I want to be alone for that.

These notes to you aren't supposed to be sad.

The thing is, life has those moments. It has to. How else can we fully appreciate the good times if we have no point of comparison?

Besides, I don't want to smudge the ink and have to begin again.

Much like my life, despite everything that has happened, I wouldn't change much if I could start over.

The main thing I would change, is that Paula would be with me for longer.

Love, Dad.'

It seems a suitable juncture for me to also call it a day. Much to my shock, it's two in the morning.

Who knows where the time goes?

A slight feeling of depression accompanies me, as I depress the power switch on the amp, having remembered to turn the volume down.

The platter ceases rotating, and I close the lid on my day.

In the morning, I'll make a cup of tea for one.

And I'll begin again.

21.

'00282 - Cat Stevens - Matthew And Son'.

'Me again, Danny. And so soon!

I'm sorry I was a bit glum in my last note. But life isn't perfect, and so there have to be those times.

How can we hang on to a dream? I'll answer the question. Through our memories, son. And these records, at the risk of repeating myself, hold every single one of them for me.

We jumped to 1967 fairly quickly. The final quarter of '66 wasn't my most upbeat. There was no inclination to discover anything new. That was true of music, and life more broadly.

In addition, I had the business to focus on. Thank god that I did! It kept me occupied and stopped me thinking too much.

I was busy, Dan - as busy as I could ever recall being. As a result, I had more money in my pocket than ever before, but no time to spend it and enjoy the fruits of my labour.

Life always seems to go that way.

It's the same unwritten rule that dictates record shopping. Go when you're flush with cash, and you'll struggle to find anything to buy. Go when you're skint, and you'll see every record you've ever dreamed of owning!

The vinyl gods can be cruel, son. That said, they always seem to come up with something when it's most required.

And 1967 was a good year to be a music fan.

Though, looking at the chart, you wouldn't really know it. As I recall, when visiting a shop in Jemford Bridge early that year, it was mostly greatest hits compilations and Jim Reeves. There may even have been a Jim Reeves greatest hits compilation.

I purchased Cat Stevens because it was on the Deram label.

It became the soundtrack to those industrious times, as I lost myself in toil. Even the 'Matthew And Son' title track seemed fitting - the work's never done, working all day.

But it was 'I Love My Dog' that really impacted on me.

As a direct result of the song, I went out and got myself a dog who I named Shorty, after an Eddie Cochran track.

Of course, he wasn't short at all.

He was about six months old when I got him, and had been abandoned.

Do you remember him, Danny?

I do recall him giving you a good sniff by way of inspection when you were first born. Your mum told me to keep the dog away from you.

We were probably a little too protective when you came along. It was only because you were so precious. We didn't know if we could have any more children, so... Well, we didn't want to take any chances.

Shorty was a mix of something and labrador, and had a black coat and a solid body. And he was as smart as any dog I ever met.

He possessed a loyalty trait that I have and value. As a result, he would never run off. As long as he was where I was, he was happy. There was no need to tie him up. And he'd come to work with me every day, and lie there watching, the radio playing away.

In time, he got to know the names of certain tools! So, if I was under a car and required, say, a hammer, I'd ask him and he'd fetch it for me.

People were amazed by that.

He knew wrench and pliers, but I could never get him to learn the difference between a phillips and flat-head screwdriver. And trust me, I tried.

It was true, what Cat Stevens wrote. All the love I needed did come shining through his eyes. For a time, anyway.

He was enough. And he plugged the gaping gap in my life that had been vacated by Maddie.

His nature was gentle. I'd often wondered what he'd do if push came to shove, and something were to happen. In all honesty, I rather presumed that he didn't have a nasty bone in his body. His only way of harming anybody, would be through a boisterous greeting and an accidental topple.

Well, I was locking up one night, and it was put to the test.

Before I knew what was going on, Shorty was snarling viciously, his hackles up and his teeth bared.

That beautiful dog transformed from soft-as-silk to hard-as-nails in a blink of an eye, Dan.

I wouldn't have messed with him.

And, there he was, protectively glued to my side.

I span, my eyes taking time to adjust to the dark, and saw two men approaching.

It was evident they were trouble. One carried a hammer, and the other was there for insurance. They're always braver in numbers.

"Hammer!" I called to Shorty, and he flew through the air, all four feet off the ground, and took the hammer clean out of the man's hand.

"Drop it," I snapped. He did. It clunked to the concrete.

The other man came towards me, saying something about money.

Shorty was on him in a flash, and bowled him over on to the ground.

He went for his bloody throat, Dan. If it hadn't been for the other one going for the hammer again, I dread to think what he might have done.

"Hammer!" I said again, and Shorty tore over to where it was.

That time, he brought it to me, and sat by my side with it in his mouth.

I leaned down and took it from him.

The men skulked off, and I finished locking up before heading home in a bit of a state. I was shaking, son. It had been a pretty scary experience.

I had a bit of steak in for my tea that night. Well, I can tell you Shorty had the best piece of that!

The next day, I got a visit from the police. I was surprised, because I hadn't reported the incident.

The two clowns had only gone and reported me and Shorty for attacking them.

In the dark, I hadn't seen the extent of the damage Shorty had inflicted. The one carrying the hammer required over thirty stitches in his hand and arm, and the other had a chipped pelvis to go with lacerations to his back and legs. Claws and teeth had inflicted those.

Of course, they were claiming the attack was unprovoked, and Shorty was out of control and unrestrained.

One of the policeman looked down at the dog lying peacefully with his chin on his front paws. I think he saw the game.

Still, he had to follow up.

I gave them my version of events, as one of them fussed the dog. The other wrote it all down.

After they left, I called Ally Mac on the phone to ask his advice.

"Leave it with me," he said.

Later that day, I received another visitor. Shorty gave a low growl by way of warning.

Through the lift-up door, walked the biggest black man I've ever seen in my life.

He apologised to me for any suffering on my part. He informed me that any complaint made against me had been withdrawn, and no charges would be brought.

Further, he asked if Shorty or I had been hurt in any way, and if any damage had been done to my property.

"No," I told him.

"Good news," he drawled, in his slight Jamaican brogue, "I'm very pleased to hear no physical damage has been done to you, Mr Goods."

"Er, thank you," I replied.

He offered me a shovel of a hand to shake. I wouldn't have dared to refuse. His handshake was as solid as the rest of him, as his dark brown eyes held mine all the while.

I saw a humour lurking in those eyes, Danny. Yes, there was a hardness. But there was a confidence and a softness present, too.

"Now, it comes to my attention," he started, "that you like music, Mr Goods."

"I do. And please, call me Bill."

"Well, Bill, can you spare a couple of minutes?"

"Sure."

He opened a package he carried with him. Vinyl singles was all it contained.

"You ever hear of Desmond Dekker, Bill? Or Bob Marley? How about Lee Perry or The Skatalites?"

"No," I confessed.

"Then you know nothing about music!" he growled, before bursting into laughter.

I smiled.

He smiled back, a smile that could light the whole world up.

"These are yours, Bill. An apology. I hope you'll accept."

"Erm, thank you. It's not necessary..."

"Oh, well, in that case - how much do you want for the dog? That's a good dog, I'll tell you that for nothing. I'd love a dog like that by my side. That's insurance, right there."

"Sorry, the dog's not for sale."

"I'd lose respect for you if he was, Bill. I'm joking with you, man. Lighten up. Please take the records, and let me know what you think of them."

"Sure, " I said.

Now, I presumed he was some kind of criminal. His colour and build spoke of nightclub bouncer or drug dealer. Or both. I further took it for granted that he was an acquaintance of Baz or Ally through his line of work.

He did know Ally and Baz, and was a DJ in the clubs. But he also ran a Youth Centre in Tredmouth for kids who got into trouble, as well as those who didn't.

And he knew the two lads who had paid me a visit that night.

He coached boxing, and loved music. Just about every band to come out of Brakeshire in the sixties and seventies went through his centre. They used it for rehearsal and played their first gigs there.

And, if they had what it took, he'd farm them out to Baz, or hook them up with a London label, where he had connections.

That was how I met Darren Smith. Or Uncle Darren, as you knew him.

It was also how I first got into ska and reggae music. And an enduring passion was born.

Everything, good or bad, happens for a reason, Danny. It all leads us somewhere.

Thanks to an attempted robbery, I met my best friend. Apart from Paula, I mean. My best friend apart from Paula.

So, as my health declines, it's Darren who I wish could be with me. I wouldn't be so afraid then.

Or Shorty. I'd take Shorty being by my side.

But they're both long gone, more's the pity.

Love, Dad.'

22.

Why Darren or Shorty?

Where were my sisters and brother? They only live down the road.

It was a bit more difficult for me. But, I concede, I could have been there more for him.

Logging on, I check my social media for the first time in many days.

Not a soul has asked after my wellbeing, or sought an explanation for my absence.

I delete my account.

The phone in my hand vibrates as it chimes.

Silencing '00286 - The Doors - self-titled', the display informs me it's my work calling.

More precisely, it's Mary Charnley, head of HR. I call her Oh Dear, for her habit of saying that, but not actually meaning it.

"Hello Mary."

"Hello Daniel. How are you?"

"Not so good, as I'm sure you've heard."

"Oh dear. We were expecting you back at work this morning."

"I was hoping to be. But I'm still very weak and shaky. And in pain," I think to add.

"Oh dear, oh dear. Well, have you seen the doctor?"

"Not yet. I was just about to call and make an appointment."

I may have made that up.

"Your sign-off from work was only for two weeks, and that's expired, I'm afraid."

"Ah, yes. I've been a bit all over the place, to be honest. I think I might have done something internal. I was unconscious, you know?"

"Oh dear. It's very sad. We're all thinking of you. Did you get the card?" she asks with a certain relish.

"I did. Thank you."

"Good." It's a self-congratulatory good, that tells of having done good in the world. Obligation fulfilled.

"I'll know more when I've seen the doctor. I was going to call you then," I say. It's half true.

"Well, you must, Daniel! We need to cover your workload, and shuffle resources. Do you think you'll be in tomorrow?"

"I wouldn't have thought so."

"Oh dear. Shall we see you this week?"

"I'm not sure, Mary. As soon as I know, you'll know. It's my back, you see, I seem to have bruised my coccyx."

"Oh dear, oh dear."

"How are things at work?"

"Oh, fine, fine. The same as always. You must get an extension on the sick note, Daniel. Or your pay will be reduced. And you don't want that to happen, through no fault of your own."

"No, no. What would it get reduced to, incidentally?"

"Well, half pay after a certain time is in your contract of employment."

"Right. And how long would that run for?"

"Oh, I'm sure you'll be back with us long before that."

Don't be so fucking sure.

She fills my silence with, "oh dear. Well, call me as soon as you've seen the doctor."

"I will, Mary. Thanks for calling."

She nearly OD'd on Oh Dears there.

After hanging up the phone, I have a strong sense I shall never go back to that job.

Oh dear.

23.

I'm going to be on statins. I don't want to be. I don't want to be on anything.

Except the exercise bike. I don't mind being on that.

The only other thing I'd like to be on, is the doctor from the hospital.

My GP doesn't look like her. He's called Dr. King. Martin King. Seriously. I've always wanted to know his middle name.

I resented every second I sat in the waiting room, breathing all of the germs sick people harbour. Especially this time of year. Cold and flu season. I'll probably end up more ill as a result.

Still, that'll mean more time off work.

After talking about my blood results, and checking my joints for flexibility and pain, I inform him of my new diet and exercise regime.

He's impressed. I can tell.

"How are you in yourself? Sleeping okay? Dealing with any stress okay?" he asks me.

"Erm, yeah. I think so."

"Look, I don't see any physical reason why you can't return to work. It isn't as though you do anything strenuous. And, by your own admission, you're exercising daily."

I knew he was impressed by that.

"I have been a bit down for a while," I admit. It's the truth. Since Lisa.

"Okay. How do you cope with that?"

"We cope, don't we? We get on with life."

"You and Lisa split up, I gather."

Of course he knows about that. Lisa is his patient. He'll have seen her all through her pregnancy. Dave probably sat in this very chair. At least I won't get hair on my clothes.

"Yeah, we decided to go our separate ways."

"How are you coping with that?" he probes.

"Fine," I shrug.

"Lisa mentioned that you don't have anything to do with your family, Daniel. She was worried about you. That's all it was."

"It's none of her business, to be honest."

"No, you're right. But she does care about you, Dan."

"She should have fucking stayed, then, shouldn't she? Sorry. I didn't mean to swear."

"It's okay. Talk to me, Dan."

I don't know how to explain the way I feel.

After staring down at my slightly sweaty and interwoven hands for a few seconds, I go with, "you know when you need to fart, but you can't, because you're in a meeting or a church, or something?"

"Erm, yes."

"So you hold it in, even though it's close to escaping. And you know how, quite often, when you do that, it goes away?"

He chuckles and nods at me.

"Well, Doc, where does it go?"

"It doesn't go anywhere. It's still there. And it will come out at some point. It has to."

I nod my understanding.

He picks up my thread. "Look, I think I get the point you're making. It's not good to hold it all in. Sometimes you're better off letting rip. That said, if you could just wait until you've left my office, I'd appreciate it."

We both laugh briefly.

He continues, "it's a good analogy. You need an outlet. Don't internalise everything. Don't bottle it all up. Lisa's concern was based on that. Do you have friends, interests, a hobby?"

"The exercise bike is my main thing at the moment. And I'm eating better. Oh, and I'm playing through all of my dad's old records. I'm enjoying that."

"Good. Didn't he want them any more?"

"Ah, no. Yes, I mean. He did. But he died."

"I'm sorry to hear that."

"Ah, thanks. It was over six years ago, to be honest."

"You never mentioned it."

"Didn't I?"

He shakes his head. I've been coming for an annual physical, and a check for cancer indicators for at least ten years. Family history, and all that.

"You never answered me about having friends," he pushes.

"They aren't really friends, are they? They're all on-line. They aren't real, I suppose. It's the same with work. Take work out of the picture, and there's nothing there."

"And there's been nobody since Lisa?"

I shake my head and flash my hands out by way of saying, 'no, but what can you do? It's not through a want of wanting.'

"You know, Dan, I think there's a strong correlation between physical and mental wellbeing. We all need someone to share things with."

"You know the oddest thing?" I interject.

"Go on."

"These past couple of weeks, since I came out of hospital. I've been happier. Playing my dad's records, and discovering notes he left in them for me. It's opened me up.

I'm not sure what I'm trying to say. I've changed. I know that. Something within me has shifted. Things that I thought I cared about, no longer interest me."

"That's good. But you're going to run out of records. Then what?"

"Oh, not for a while."

"How many records are there?"

"Roughly seven and a half thousand vinyl albums."

When you say that to people, they have trouble picturing it. They go through a process of conjuring up their own record collection, from back when they were a teenager. Before they chucked them all, or donated them to charity via the local church hall jumble fundraiser.

They try to recall how many they had. Perhaps a hundred albums. Maybe even two hundred. And they depict that as a leaning stack, or a couple of cases with fold-back lids and shiny metal clips. A handle on top for carrying.

There's a brief moment where they attempt to extrapolate that image to represent seven and a half thousand. Within three seconds, they blink it away and give up.

"How long will that take you?" he asks instead.

"About five thousand hours."

I get a two week extension on my sick note.

Result!

24.

'00304 - The Hollies - Butterfly'.

'Hello again, Danny.

People talk about 1967 with such reverence.

The truth is, for the first half of the year, I only heard the music through the radio. It was all singles, and, as you know, that wasn't my thing. Albums that captured the time didn't begin to hit the shops until the summer.

But I was acutely aware of a change in the wind.

I wasn't ready to embrace it. It was anything but a Summer of Love for me.

I was plodding around, sulking about Madeleine, and generally feeling sorry for myself.

As August and September came and went, I picked up the albums you've just played. But my heart wasn't in them.

To this day, I regret it. I missed Pink Floyd's 'Piper At The Gates Of Dawn' as a result of my mood. You'll find it a few records from now, as I eventually got a copy in 1968.

Albums took over from singles at that time, I suppose. They became more cohesive - more works of art, rather than a bunch of singles and other songs thrown on to a record.

New labels sprang up. Either independently, or as sub-labels of major imprints, such as Deram. Really, though, Deram was simply the London American Recordings of its day. The only real difference being, most of the acts were from the UK.

No sooner had the Summer Of Love passed me by, than I picked up The Hollies 'Butterfly' and snapped to attention.

If you count back, I'd only added eighteen albums to my collection since the February. And, for the first time, I had surplus cash to spend.

Madeleine walking out of my life had extinguished a flame in me. Or, at least, hidden it for a while.

But from this point on, my passion was reignited like never before.

If I had records, I could deal with anything life might throw at me. With my vinyl, I could thrive. I would never be lonely. I would never be alone.

It became clear to me, that any depression I felt was overcome by music. It set my mood. It levelled me out when I required that, and it lifted me as necessary. It allowed me to grieve and celebrate, to relax and rejoice. And now, sitting here many years on, it allows me to recall all of the important moments in my life.

So, this is an introduction, really, Dan. This is the beginning of the next most glorious chapter of my life.

More on which, next time!

Love, Dad.'

'00305 - Incredible String Band - 5000 Spirits Or The Layers Of The Onion'.

'00306 - The Bee Gees - Bee Gees 1st'.

How strange to hear The Bee Gees as they were in 1967. I've only ever known the disco based singles from the seventies. 'Saturday Night Fever', to put it in a nutshell.

Blossom Toes, Cream, Kaleidoscope.

Kaleidoscope is the band! 'Tangerine Dream' is the title! Oh, thank fuck!

Out of interest, I look it up on the internet, as I recall the Van Man gazing at it as though he wanted to have sex with it.

It's mono on Fontana.

A grand.
Cheeky fucker.

25.

Sixteen days in, and I can hold her steady at twenty-five kilometers per hour on the bike. For about fifteen minutes.

A quarter of an hour is all I have before the side of the record can finish. I dismount, mop the sweat from my hair, and get ready to turn or change the record.

Three pairs of exercise trousers, and four breathable mesh t-shirts arrive in the post. It is my new uniform.

I call work, and have a brief chat with Mary Charnley. Two more weeks of freedom are mine. Well, twelve days, seeing how it's Tuesday afternoon.

'Tuesday Afternoon'.

The Moody Blues, I know, because I played it this very morning.

'Days Of Future Passed'.

Reading Dad's notes is a bit like that. It's the past, but I'm looking forward to reading about his future.

What does my future hold?

What will I do in two weeks time, when my sick note expires?

More vitally, what will work do if I simply don't go back? Can they dismiss me? Can I survive on half pay?

I'm spending less, despite the newly acquired attire.

No more lunchtime pints and bus fare. No more expensive junk food lunches, and taxis home when it rains and I can't face the bus. No more shirts and suits to dry-clean. No more daft coffees with froth and sprinkles. No more buying technology and subscribing to memberships. No more all-channel with added sports tiers satellite telly subscription. No more on-line gambling and gaming. No more take-aways at night because I'm too knackered to cook myself something.

On the list goes.

Yes, I can survive on half pay. Half pay enables me a full life.

But they won't pay me, even half, for ever. They expect something in return. The rent needs to be paid. The bills, too.

And the debts. They require clearing. The interest payments are crippling me.

It's the debts that bind me. Take them away, and I can just about survive.

Presumably, I'll get some kind of financial package from work if I force their hand. I've been there for over fifteen years. I wonder how much it will be. Enough to clear those arrears?

I'm not even five percent of the way through my dad's record collection. Box number four is just about done with. Ninety-four to go.

I totted them up when listening to 'South Pacific', which probably says a great deal about the album.

And it was number one on the chart for years.

If it wasn't for The Beatles, it might still be number one today.

I'm probably, all things considered, going to need a part-time job doing something.

A grand for that Kaleidoscope album keeps flashing through my mind.

A grand would buy me a month, if I tighten my belt. And all of this cycling means my belt is indeed tightened.

The thing is, I really like that album. 'The Sky Children' blew me away. It's childlike and beautiful and pure.

It made me think of mum singing to me when I was little.

She may have even sung that song. I can't remember.

No, I'm keeping that one.

I'm keeping them all.

But it is worth a grand...

And dad did write that they are mine to do with as I please.

People say that. It doesn't mean that they mean it.

I know, deep down, that he wanted me to cherish these records, just as he did.

But he also wanted me to be true to myself, and to be my own person. The records were his thing, not mine.

I didn't have a thing. Not really. All of my things were there to kill time and stave off boredom. They were slightly better than doing nothing.

Do nothing for too long, and you'll end up doolally.

I can't cycle for ever. I need other activities.

Cranking up the volume, I begin clearing the front room of all contents apart from my comfy leather recliner.

The only reason the flat-screen television survives the cull, is because I have no idea how to take it down from the wall. I imagine it may involve the use of at least one tool.

It may even be a two-man job, and I am but one man. Alone. But not lonely. Not any more.

I've met all of these characters that fill my life. Their satanic majesties, Simon Simopath, Mr Fantasy, all heading up the junction for some supernatural fairy tales.

Before I know what's what, it's tomorrow, and a revolution has taken place. My time has come.

And my white exercise bicycle sits in the middle of it all.

Dad's... My turntable has pride of place, the speakers on the sturdy side units where heretofore leaning stacks of DVDs and computer games stood.

Boxes five and six are downstairs, ready to be explored.

I carried them all by myself!

The spare room is no longer spare. It is now the Record Room. Shelving is due to arrive by the end of the week. More debt. Some records will go down here, but there isn't enough wall space. So some will remain upstairs.

I can do this.

And I know how I'll buy my freedom for a while.

It came to me in a flash, and I couldn't believe it took me so long to think of it.

I'm going to release the missing Tommy Histon LP.

I have the only two copies in existence. And one has never been played.

The demand is there. I saw it on the internet. The vinyl revival. Histon's cult status.

It's perfect timing.

Now, how in the name of all things sacred do you go about doing that?

26.

A box within the box confronts me.

'00369 - Donovan - A Gift From A Flower To A Garden'.

Inside, lying on top of the records, I find a folded letter, my dad's familiar hand on show.

'Hello son.

I left you alone for a while to enjoy the music. It really was a glorious time. I hope you can appreciate what it was like living through it.

I was simply buying records unheard and unknown, based solely on the sleeve art being right. Just about everything I got was a winner.

This is one of those records where I know the moment I got it. I didn't buy it. It's an American pressing that was available a few months before it was released in the UK.

It came to me on Saturday March 16th, 1968, at approximately five in the evening.

Notice the slight water damage on one edge of the box, where it stood in the rain awaiting my return from work.

Well, I was perplexed, son. Where had it come from? I hadn't ordered it. My first thought was Ally Mac. So I called him, but he knew nothing of it.

Darren was my second port of call. Again, I drew a blank.

It took me a while to get to the record. I had hands to wash, and shopping to put away. Shorty needed feeding. A beer needed drinking. Shorty loved a bit of beer in his bowl after his dinner.

It was the end of the week, son, and I was worn out.

Eventually, I put the record on - the first of the two albums inside. 'Wear Your Love Like Heaven' kicked off as I sank into the tub.

And I again wondered how that LP came to be there.

After my bath, I dried myself and went to change the record. At the bottom, beneath the two white paper-sleeved albums, I discovered an orange folder with Donovan printed on the front.

Opening it, I leafed through the coloured card sheets with cartoon pictures and lyrics on. It was a thing of beauty, the like of which I'd never seen before.

A small piece of paper fell out. On it was 'Assembled by', and a stamp with a four digit number and a date of December 2nd, 1967. It was all part of the package.

I sifted through those inserts, and handwritten on the reverse of one was, 'I'm looking for a garden where I can plant myself and be for the rest of my life. I'm sorry for leaving. I had to be sure. And now I am. I'm sure that I love you'.

Tucked in the sleeve for the second record, I discovered a small photo of Madeleine Michey.

Except it wasn't her.

It was someone very like her.

She wore no make-up, the dark liner not present, and her lips were soft and pink, not harsh and red.

Similarly soft and welcoming were the warm brown eyes that looked half-mirthfully into the lens.

Gone was the black hair, replaced by a natural wavy light brown.

It's the hair and eyes that you inherited, Dan.

On the back was written, 'Paula x'.

And a phone number.

I called it immediately. Somebody answered. It was a hotel near Jemford Bridge called The Bridgehouse.

I asked for Madeleine Michey. They'd never heard of her. There was nobody staying there with that name.

"Paula?" I asked next.

There was a pause.

"Do you have a surname?"

"Paula Michey?" I tried.

"There's nobody here by that name, sir."

Shit!

I drove there, arriving about eight o'clock. It was pissing down, the same rain that had spoiled the box on the Donovan record.

All I could think to do was order a beer and wait in the small bar area. I positioned myself so I was looking out into the foyer.

For an hour and a quarter, I sat there nursing my pint.

She came down for a drink at nine fifteen, having sat by the phone awaiting my call.

I watched her all the way, but she didn't see me at first, the dimness in the bar shrouding me.

I walked up behind her as she ordered a glass of wine, and I handed the money to the barman before she could put it on her room.

Cool as you like, she turned, smiled, and asked, "aren't you having one?"

"I have to drive back to Palmerton Chase."

"No you don't," she told me, and tipped her head slightly to one side, "I have the room for one night."

"I'll have to get back for Shorty in the morning," I mused out-loud.

"Shorty?"

"My dog."

She beamed at that revelation.

"We've not met. I'm Paula," she introduced herself, and offered me a hand.

I took it, and never let go.

I held that hand every day for the next fifteen years. I held it as she gave birth to our children. Well, one of you, anyway.

And I held it as she fought so hard against the cancer, Danny.

For half of that night in the hotel, we talked. We talked until we fell asleep.

She'd gone away for a while, Dan. She went and pursued her modeling career, and worked out what she wanted from life.

"I needed to be certain, Bill. If I hadn't gone, I would have spent the rest of my life wondering 'what if?'. And now I have no doubts. I've tried that, and it isn't what I want. I choose you. If you'll have me."

We were married within three months. She fell pregnant six months after. And Trevor was born in the late-summer of 1969.

And I was, for all of the time I was with her, the happiest man in the world.

Her note, by the way? It was what gave me the notion of leaving notes in records for you, Dan.

That picture of your mum is at the bottom of the box. As is the note she left for me that day.

They're yours now. They should have been yours long before now. You deserve to know the history.

I'm sorry I kept it from you.

I wanted it all to myself.

The truth is, I was terrified of sharing it. If I did that, it would dilute it. It would lessen my memory of her.

It would provoke questions requiring answers, and it would have become about you.

I wanted it to be about me and Paula. And once Paula was no longer alive, I wanted it to be about me.

I hope you can forgive me for being a selfish old man.

I have always loved you.

Love, Dad.'

Carefully removing all of the contents of the box, I notice the water mark on the dark blue spine.

Turning each card in turn, I find my mum's message on the back of the eighth, 'Widow With Shawl'.

I wonder why she chose that one. The lyrics printed on the other side hold no meaning, as far as I can tell.

My finger traces her handwriting.

Just as it traces her face on the photograph.

And I know it's time for me to go to bed. But I can't. I have to play the second LP in the box.

My mum would sing to me when she put me to bed. She may have sung these songs.

I was too young to remember.

Nobody sang to me after she died.

Despite my dad playing records all the time, there was no music I cared to hear if it didn't emanate from my mother's mouth.

27.

Another day. Another year.

My parents were buying at least one record a week through 1968.

The Zombies, Rainbow Ffolly, Small Faces, The Crazy World Of Arthur Brown.

Fairport Convention, July, Davy Graham, Lee Hazlewood.

Scott Walker, Simon And Garfunkel, The Moody Blues.

I lose myself in the music, preparing my dinner to one side of an LP, and eating it to the other.

Thursday comes and goes. I resent the time it takes to shower and dry myself. It feels like a waste. But I must clean my body, and remove the constant film of sweat that coats my skin as I continue to obdurately pedal the bike.

The Beatles, Tyrannosaurus Rex, The Status Quo - I've heard of them.

Soft Machine, Caravan, The Idle Race.

Leonard Cohen, Frank Sinatra, Jethro Tull.

Other artists reappear - Eddie Cochran, The Everly Brothers, and a wonderful record by Del Shannon called 'The Further Adventures Of Charles Westover'.

Motown, ska, soul and blues records pepper throughout, and change the mood and feel.

It's the variety that is the spice of their life.

The Good The Bad And The Ugly and The Pretty Things.

'SF Sorrow'.

There are no notes amidst the notes, as 1968 draws to a close.

It frustrates me, but I understand it. This was their time before settling down and having a family. If my parents had a glory year, it was 1968. And, I reason, it's none of my business.

Still, I can't help but wonder what they looked like and did. Using my phone, I find a site that describes the weather that year.

It was dull and wet with a miserable late-summer. Grey skies and black roads were the scene, somewhat at odds with a lot of the sounds they were listening to.

In my mind, I'd depicted my happily hippily beautiful mum in a white summer dress, flowers in her hair, walking the Brake Hills to the north, or Border Ridge to the south. It offers a perfect lush green backdrop, with a deep solid blue sky above, replete with yellow sun with a happy face on it, lighting up her fair hair and tanning her pale skin.

Dad would have grown his dark brown hair over his collar, a bit like Paul McCartney, not daring to go full-on Lennon. More practical for work that way. His shirt would be open a couple of buttons at the neck, just sufficient to show the beginnings of his chest hair. For some reason, I gave him a moustache like Lee Hazlewood, because I think it would have suited him.

They'd walk along the crest of the hills, my parents, Nancy and Lee, hand in hand, arm in arm, all virginal innocence. Because my mental image of Paula is not how it was for Madeleine Michey.

Not since she became my mother.

That not-so-summery weather summary I discovered has forced me to change my imaginings.

To be honest, it probably explains why they bought so many records. It was their entertainment as the rain lashed down outside.

I see them - mum and dad, Nancy and Lee - on a sofa, a grey and tempestuous sky the scene out of a window, as they hold one another and listen to the music thrumming forth from my father's cabinet housed hi-fi.

Their hands hold cups of steaming liquid, their fingers threaded through the handles.

The scene shifts in my mind. They're on the move.

A sudden downpour has them running through the street, him covering her head with his coat, as she snuggles against him, a record in his other hand, his priorities right.

They're laughing in my snapshot, their mouths wide and eyes bright, as the drops explosively bounce off the coat, and they leap together over a puddle.

It doesn't matter. Nothing matters as long as they're together.

I've never known that.

Ah, perhaps I did. For the first few weeks with Lisa. But it quickly went off the boil.

Rain would make her hair frizz.

Happy birthday, I think to myself.

I am thirty-nine today.

She was thirty-nine when she died.

I got three cards. One each from my brother and sisters. They still bother, despite my never reciprocating.

Lisa didn't send one.

The cards stand on the media cabinet, either side of a speaker. I kept the 'Get Well Soon' card from work to pad it out a bit.

I think of a photograph.

Me on my mum's knee. Our lips pursed with blowing, as though we were blowing a kiss.

A candle just extinguished, as a wisp of smoke curls up from the wick. The only evidence that it was once aflame.

This balloon burning.

My first birthday.

Where is that smoke now? What became of it? Surely it must still exist in diluted form.

If I could find it, and capture it, it will still contain the mingled breaths of my mother and I, as she helped me blow that candle out.

I can't. It's impossible.

The final track on the final side of the final record they bought in 1968 draws to a close.

The old man is gone.

Leaving me as the loneliest person.

28.

1969 begins with '00414 - Sam Gopal - Escalator'.

Desmond Dekker, I decide, is immense.

Dusty Springfield, Tim Buckley, Leonard Cohen, Elton John, Joni Mitchell.

I have a feeling that mum picked some of the purchases.

My cycling slows as the pace drops through the year. These are people I've heard of. They still get played on the BBC.

Dad's record buying habit was noticeably curtailed through the year, as, I presume, money was required for other more pressing matters.

It was the year my parents bought and moved to the house in which I was born. That was just before Trevor appeared in the world.

Dad would live in that house for the rest of his life.

It comes as no surprise to find a note in September of 1969.

'00433 - Nick Drake - Five Leaves Left'.

'Dear Dan,

It's been a year and a half since I wrote to you, even though it was only four days ago in my time.

And it was my time, son.

I wonder how long it took you to get through those sixty-four albums since my last letter. Did you skip any? I hope not, because it was a very good year in music terms.

It was a very good year in every sense.

I haven't mentioned live music much, have I?

The truth is, I always preferred the studio recordings to the live experience. Money wasn't limitless, so I chose my path.

For me, a record was permanent, whereas a show lasted for a couple of hours. Does that make sense?

Yes, of course I still fondly recall that Cochran-Vincent gig in 1960, but as much for the other events that took place as the concert itself.

All of that said, we were attending shows regularly. At least once a month, we'd head over to Tredmouth to support Darren's bands at the Youth Centre, or to catch a bigger name in one of Baz Baxter's clubs.

Paula had seen the top names, such as Pink Floyd and Cream, when she was in London.

Only once did we make a trek to the capital together, to see The Soft Machine at The Roundhouse.

Mostly, I remember the dancers, and the film and light show. Ally Mac got us in for free.

Which was a good job, as a night in a grotty hotel cost all of our budget.

I was a bit out of my depth, son, having rarely left Brakeshire. But Paula knew a few faces, so we got to hang out with some probably quite important people in the music business.

Half of my night was spent chatting to a man about seeing Eddie Cochran and Gene Vincent in 1960, and the merits of Tommy Histon. To this day, I have no idea who he was. And he was pretty smashed on drugs.

The other half was taken up by a woman who, as far as I could understand things, wanted to have sex with me and Paula at the same time.

It didn't happen.

I also declined the offer to take whatever drugs she was taking in vast quantities.

Paula had taken some harder drugs, including LSD, when she was in London the year before. She hadn't enjoyed the experience, so I always left it alone. It was around, though, even in Brakeshire, but it never appealed.

Smoking marijuana was as hard-core as we ever got together. And that was easy to come by. I didn't need much more, as the music always gave me enough of a buzz.

That's the thing with drugs, and even drink. I never much felt the urge, as the experience didn't require enhancing. I was perfectly content with my life as it was - Paula, my records and my work.

It bothered me, after the night in London, as to what Paula may have got up to when she was away from me for that year and a half.

She'd always say it wasn't really her. That it happened to someone else - Madeleine Michey.

She wasn't a virgin when I met her in 1966, and I know she had relationships after she left that year.

We'd argue about it, Dan. It was stupid, now I can look back on it. But I was young, and not terribly experienced.

All of those hours I spent sulking over it, and the days of not talking.

Do you know what I would give to get the time back?

There were so many things over the years that would annoy me.

Paula would dry her hair in this particular way. She'd apply short bursts from the dryer, and clank it down on the counter while she brushed. Repeat. And repeat. And bloody repeat. Over and over again.

I'd lie in bed, and feel myself getting wound up by it. By the time she appeared, I'd be feigning sleep so she wouldn't see that I was pissed off.

So many nights were wasted because of that.

And it was all so bloody trivial!

How I longed to hear the hairdryer when she lost all of her hair to the chemo, Dan.

And how I'd give a limb and every record I own right now, just to have her drying her hair in the bathroom.

Watch out for that, son. Think about every minute. And try not to waste one of them, because life is so short.

Ah, but back to 1969. We were gigging regularly, and generally having a whale of a time.

However, things were about to change. We were both twenty-six that year, and decided to buy a house. We'd talked about having children, so knew we'd need a place large enough to accommodate a family.

It meant bunkering down and saving for the deposit, and ensuring we could manage the repayments once we had it. My business was steady, thanks to Ally and Baz, plus the regular customers I'd built up in Palmerton Chase.

But it wasn't enough.

Paula got a job as a sales assistant in a clothing shop in Drescombe, and worked there until she was about to pop with Trevor. She'd get the bus back and forth every day for the first few months.

For my part, I took extra work delivering jukebox records to pubs and cafes all over Brakeshire in the evenings. It was the best time to catch the pubs when they were open, so it tied in with my garage work.

Shorty would come with me in a van Ally let me use. It saved time, as I didn't have to lock up. Nobody would go near the van with Shorty on patrol.

Paula passed her driving test in July, so could take the car to work and back when she was most heavily pregnant.

And he was heavy, your brother. An ounce over ten pounds! And he was stubborn. He didn't want to come out.

Trevor was, in his beginning, what he is right now, Dan. All of you demonstrated traits of personality immediately, that would characterise you as you got older.

Trevor likes what he knows. He doesn't handle change well. He would have been perfectly happy to stay in the womb for ever.

It's why I'm leaving him the business, Dan.

I hope you weren't upset by my choices.

On paper, it looks as though you got the worst end of the deal. However, by now, if you've been paying proper attention, you actually got the best of it.

Goods Vehicles isn't worth very much, Danny. That's the truth. The ramps and winches might sell for a few grand. The tools for a few more. The premises are leased, and the business has been struggling for years.

To be honest, by the time I stepped away, and Trev took it on, I was barely paying myself a wage. The money wasn't there.

Ally and Baz were no more, though Baz's son would always pass a bit of work our way.

Generally, though, the world changed.

New cars are the thing. And when people buy new cars, they get a dealership service contract, free oil changes, and years of warranty.

So few people keep a car long enough for it to expire, so the trade never reaches the small man on the street. The folk who own those older cars generally can't afford to pay much by way of repair. If they could, they'd have a new car.

Classic car owners do a lot of the work themselves these days, as a hobby or through a club. The internet has enabled that.

Punctures, batteries and plugs and points are what we spent most of our time working on. And there isn't much money to be had in that, because the chains can undercut us. We needed to be competitive.

Patching up MOT failures has been our trade for years. A plate welded, an exhaust replaced, a bulb changed, or wheels aligned.

It's a few quid here, and a few quid there.

Trevor's constantly having to retrain, to stay current, as technology pervades more and more. Being a car mechanic is more like being a computer repair person these days.

He's getting twenty grand a year out of it, Danny. And having to work sixty hours a week, minimum, for that. I was earning that much in 1985 when Trev came to work for me. So it's not even half as much, given inflation.

He earned the business, as hard as it is to make a crust from.

When Paula died, he left school as soon as he could to come and work with me. And even before then, he worked evenings, weekends and school holidays. In fact, for his last year of schooling, Trev missed more time than he attended. Without Trevor, I dread to think what might have happened to us all.

There was talk about you kids going off to live with relatives. As it was, you were farmed off to aunts and uncles half the time.

The rest of the time, you sat with me in my room as I played my records and worked out how on earth I was going to cope.

What I failed to see, was that I was coping by doing that.

You were happy enough, playing on the carpet, humming away to the songs.

Similarly, your sisters need the house between them. They have so little, Danny. And they each have children of their own.

Besides which, I had to borrow against it later on in life, so there isn't as much there as you might have thought.

As I wrote before, you were the one I never had to worry about. You got away, and have a career - a proper profession, I might term it. You're a manager, and the world will always need those. As technology takes over, it shall always require managing.

And you're qualified, with a degree in chemistry, and certificates and courses attended.

Trevor has nothing if he doesn't have the garage.

Beth and Yvonne have very little if you take away their husbands' income. And what little they have is spent on their children.

And they are both so giving - a trait they inherited from my Aunt Bet - that they deprive themselves all the time. Both had to become, to some degree, a mother to you. They would have been off living their lives, but they stayed with me, and helped out, as they did their bit to keep us all together.

We are a family, Dan, because of the sacrifices you all had to make.

You are the success story to come from it. Because of the roles played by your brother and sisters, you were able to be educated. You were free to move away, to university, and the city of Tredmouth, where you run the local paper.

Through that, you met Lisa, and enjoy the bright lights as a professional couple. And we're all so proud of you for what you've achieved.

It makes the sacrifices worthwhile.

But back to Nick Drake.

Trevor was born at home, in the bedroom above my head as I sit here writing away.

I paced the room, as the labour went on for twenty-one hours. Twenty-one bloody hours!

The music remained silent at first, as I listened to the comings and goings above me.

I'd walk out in the garden when the screams got too bad.

I was terrified, son. Terrified of something going wrong up there, and utterly petrified of the responsibility of being a father.

To Paula, I put on a brave face, but underneath, I doubted my ability to cope.

In a lull, after twenty hours of fretting and pacing, I heard Paula call my name.

Now, this was before the days of father's being present at the birth, so I presumed it was all over.

I ran up the stairs, and entered the room.

It was during a break in the contractions.

She held her hand out to me.

Advancing, I took it in mine, the sweat clammy on both of us.

She was blowing breaths out of her mouth, her hair matted to her forehead.

She tugged me towards her.

Leaning, I turned my ear to her mouth.

She said, "will you play some fucking music, Bill! I can't do it with you listening!"

I went down and cranked up the volume. I don't know what I played, but I played it loud. And it was rock. Perhaps it was The Aynsley Dunbar Retaliation, now that I think of it.

It was loud enough so I didn't hear the midwife come down the stairs.

She appeared as I changed the record to my latest acquisition. I'd decided something soft and gentle, something soothing and beautiful might serve the purpose better. My aim was to get Paula to relax.

The needle descended, and I turned to see a portly lady with a bundle in her arms.

I sat down, and she handed me Trevor.

In my haste, I'd put side two on first, so 'Cello Song' was the first track he sat with me and listened to.

Staring down, I saw this pinky-yellow face looking out from a white cotton shroud.

I could recognise myself in his countenance.

That Nick Drake LP didn't leave the deck for the rest of the day.

And when the day was done, and the evening came on, I lay on the bed with Paula and our newborn son.

As we listened to the album again and again - a record I would have adored even without the circumstances under which I first heard it - I just knew I would be fine.

Look after your brother, son. I know he's the elder. But you owe him for all he did and sacrificed for you.

And you're simply better equipped to look out for him than he is for you.

Love, Dad.'

29.

An email to a bloke called Colin was met with derision, as he felt the need to point out that the demo acoustic takes of Tommy Histon's final album, 'Kimono For Kip', are readily available, and have been reissued many times since the sixties.

I pointed out that these were the finished tracks from the studio at Norton Bassett.

"Who finished them?" he sneered.

"He did. My father knew him. He was his driver when he came to England to record it in '64."

I mentioned Ally Mac and Baz Baxter, the owners of Chemisette Records. I slipped in that they were friends of my father's. He was suddenly more attentive.

He rang me, and I played the first track down the line to him.

Questions were being fired at me, so I made an excuse and got off the phone.

Since then, my email has been going crazy.

Colin connected me with a man called Keith, who put me in touch with a Tony, who insisted John was the man to go to with this.

John turned out to be John Greene, who runs the Tommy Histon Appreciation Society, based in Chester.

I don't know why it's based there. Presumably because it's where John Greene lives.

He insisted on ringing me. And again, I played him the opening track down the phone.

Publishing rights seem to be an issue.

I know a bit about that from work, where pictures are used in articles. A fee often needs to be paid, and a credit given.

As a result, we tend to always use pictures from the agency the parent company subscribes to.

An organisation called the Performing Right Society, and another called the Mechanical-Copyright Protection Society, have been contacted by John to, "test the water, and see where we are with regard to ownership."

"I own it."

Apparently, it isn't that straightforward.

And it may take a while to get to the bottom of.

There's a level of scepticism in his tone. Is he trying to scare me, or test my sincerity via the cunning use of copyright infringement?

"How much are you looking to get for it?" he asks.

"It's not for sale. I want to release it as a record."

"Okay. What sort of scale are you thinking?"

"A few hundred LPs, I suppose. It's for my dad, really. And to get some money while I play all of his records."

"Ah, so it's your dad's record. Can I speak to him?"

"Are you a medium?"

"Erm, no, large. Have you got t-shirts?"

"What? Why would I need a t-shirt?"

"Oh, a medium! So, he's dead. I'm sorry."

"It was over six years ago. But I found the record. It was in his collection. Along with a letter explaining it all."

"Right. Can I see the letter?"

"Not really. It's personal."

"Perhaps you could write the gist of it for the album, if it ever gets that far?"

"I could. I write for the local paper sometimes."

"You haven't written about the album, have you?"

"No. I'm off work since I had a tumble. That's why I'm playing the records."

"Erm..."

"Don't worry about it. Yes, I'll write something up for the record."

"We need to prove that this is Tommy Histon, and not something added afterwards. It needs provenance. That means..."

"I know what it means," I interrupt, a narky tone in my voice, "I also know what the record's all about. Do you have the demo versions?"

"Yes, of course." He's a bit more respectful now.

"Well, I can explain it all. It'll sound as mad as a fish playing cricket when I do, but I can tell you what the record is based on. I know how he came up with the album title, and it has little or nothing to do with Ally Mac wearing a kimono."

"Well, that's on good authority..."

"It may be a factor, but it isn't at the heart of it. As for the song lyrics, start by looking at the 1964 Grand National."

"The what?"

"The 1964 Grand National."

"Right, erm, I have to, erm, take another call."

He thinks I'm a loony.

"No problem," I reply, keen to get on with my record playing day.

I thought it best to hold back on the potassium permanganate reference.

In my mind, I can picture John Greene. I see him end the call, switch to the internet, and search for the National. His eyes widen as he reads through the runners, and spots a note about a plane crash. The victim's names are the final piece of the puzzle.

He runs, sifting through records or CDs, looking for the Histon demos.

He puts it on, the National information still open in front of him.

And he simply listens.

He becomes more and more agitated and restless as each reference reveals itself. The checking was unnecessary, as he knows the lyrics intimately, but he had to be certain.

It proves that I know something. And what intrigues him the most, is how do I know? Because, really, there's only one way I could know.

It's because I'm legitimate in all I claim.

Twelve minutes is all it takes for him to call me back. He barely made it half way through one side.

"Apologies for that, Danny."

We're best fucking mates now.

"No problem."

"You're right. Everything you said, was right!"

"I know."

"The record you have - is it a proper record, pressed as a test-pressing? Or is it an acetate?"

"I don't know the difference," I admit.

"An acetate is a thin layer of vinyl laid over a metal disc. They're called lacquers. It's the step before the vinyl goes to production, in order to test the transfer from tape before the stampers are made, which are then used to press the record."

"It did feel different. So it may be an acetate. Is that good or bad?"

"It's not necessarily a problem as long as it hasn't been played too many times. They do tend to deteriorate quite quickly."

"I honestly believe that it's never been played."

"Brilliant!"

He's getting keener by the minute.

He adds, "if it has never been played, how did you play it to Colin and myself?"

"Oh, there are two copies. One for playing, and one to be kept. Those were Tommy's instructions to my dad."

"So, the other is absolutely mint?" His voice went a bit squeaky when he asked that.

"As far as I know. Like I say, I haven't played it."

"So, a needle-drop could potentially recreate it, if it was done professionally."

"I don't know what that means. I'd be reluctant to drop a needle on it."

He laughs.

"Have you shared the tracks with anybody?" John asks, somewhat warily.

"No."

"Then don't. In fact, don't even play them down the phone to anyone. And keep the record in a safe place."

"Will do."

"Okay, Danny. Thanks. This is not what I expected to happen today. In fact, I never thought this would happen in my lifetime. I'm in a state of shock, to be honest. I'm all over this right now. Today! Look, I'll be in touch as soon as we know where we are with the rights."

"Great."

"And you may want to think about a few thousand LPs, as well as a general worldwide CD and download release."

"Okay. The more the merrier."

"I won't lie to you, Danny. If this is real, people will pay tens of thousands for those records you have."

"They're not for sale," I reiterate.

"Okay. Anyway, let's not get ahead of ourselves. There's a lot of work to be done in authenticating, not to mention the rights issues."

"By the way," I volunteer, "the run-off groove is etched."

"What does it say?" he asks.

"CH-770001, which I think is the Chemisette Records release number."

John Greene gives a little happy whimper at that. Like a dog looking at a biscuit being eaten by a human.

I continue. "And then, '2B, 4D, postP' is hand-etched."

"What do you make of that?"

Suddenly, I'm the authority.

"It's probably coincidence, but my dad was Bill, I'm Danny, and my mum was called Paula."

"Well, it could be that. After all, he knew your father well enough to give him the records."

"The thing is, it was a couple of years before he met my mum."

"Right."

"And I wouldn't be born for another sixteen years."

"Shit. You do know that he believed he could see the future?"

"Yes, my dad mentioned that."

"And is Paula, your mother... Is she also deceased?"

"Yes. Many years ago."

"I'm sorry."

"Thanks."

"Shit."

"I know."

"Speak soon, Danny."

"Yep."

All things considered, I think that went well.

30.

A new decade to explore.

The sixties ended with, aptly enough, '00440 - The End - Introspection'.

Discovering a letter almost immediately, comes as an unexpected, but pleasant, surprise. It's not long since dad last wrote.

'00443 - Syd Barrett - The Madcap Laughs'.

As is my quickly established routine, I begin the record before mounting the bike, or settling in my chair, to read. In this instance, the latter.

Within a few seconds, I understand why dad wrote about this one. From the first lyric, it becomes clear the song is known to me.

But I could never have recalled what it was, or who it was by.

It was by my mum, as far as I've always been concerned.

'Terrapin' I learn, by glancing at the sleeve.

She'd sing it to me, and act out a little game. I'd mimic her, but could never get all of the words. I could only form certain phrases.

'I really love you,' she'd sing at me, a finger pointed gently at my chest.

We'd bump noses and swim like fishes before smiling up at the sunlight.

The dodge a tooth refrain was why she did it, as I was teething, and the song and routine made me forget about the pain.

And she'd tell me that her hair was on end about me, her baby.

She sang that even though she didn't have any. It would make her laugh, her mouth wide, her breath warm on my face.

It was later. Much later. A few years after mum was gone, I snuck into my dad's room and went through all of his records looking for this one.

I'd lost a tooth the day before, and it had summoned forth a memory I didn't know I held.

A tooth for a tooth, as I gave up the one that had burst from my gum that day six or seven years before, when my mum sang to me and bumped noses and laughed about not having any hair to stand on end.

All I wanted to do was to hear the song again.

My tongue rests on the tooth that replaced it. I recall which one it was. Top, just left of the middle two.

Dad caught me in his room, about to play the track.

He made me jump, and I dropped the tonearm, the needle falling down and hitting the vinyl with a vicious clunk and scrape, before jumping in the air and bouncing across the surface like a flat pebble across a lake.

I tried to catch it, but succeeded only in dragging the tip back over the reflective black playing surface.

In the light, I could see the damage I'd done.

"Leave it! Get out!" dad barked at me.

I open the letter and read.

'Hello Dan.

Syd Barrett was Paula's favourite. She fell for his music with Pink Floyd in London before they even had a record out.

If you recall, I almost missed 'Piper At The Gates Of Dawn' because I was so heartbroken at her leaving.

Maybe I avoided it because I knew how much she would like it. It was the opposite of what I did with Mags all those years before.

I don't know if you remember, because you were quite young, but you scratched this record one day when you were eight or nine or so.

You were doing what kids do, and meddling where you shouldn't have been. Anyway, I caught you, and you dropped the needle on it!

Sorry I shouted.

As you will have noticed, I always looked after my records. I was a bit obsessive about them. I still am.

So, yes, I was pissed off at you, son.

Yet, here's the thing with that.

In the twenty-five years since you scratched it, I've smiled every time I've heard the little click the scratch makes.

In fact, I've bought at least two reissues of the album since then, but they don't sound right without that flaw.

The memories aren't only contained in the music, Dan.

They also exist in the physical item. The oily thumbprint on Jackson C Frank. A bent corner on a cover from where Yvonne placed a Christmas present on top of the record. A puncture mark on another sleeve, where Shorty got a bit carried away. Red wine on an album, where I had a few too many celebrating Paula's thirtieth. A coffee cup ring on another, thanks to Beth. A slight warp when Paula left an album in the back of the car in the direct sunlight.

Countless other imperfections, inflicted by life and circumstances.

And this scratch on Syd Barrett's 'The Madcap Laughs' is another.

I was angry at all those mishaps, but I laugh at them now.

Each one I encounter brings back a memory that makes me chortle away to myself.

Every defect tells a story - the story of our life.

And it's joyous, all of it. Contained within, is my family, and every single thing that is precious to me.

All these records really are, Dan? They're a shortcut to memories.

It's a good record, though, eh? You shouldn't have touched it without asking!

I'll write again soon, son. The doctor is due in a few minutes, so I have to dash.

Well, maybe not dash. But I need to shuffle off and use the toilet.

See you.

Dad x.'

I listen to the click on each rotation, as the stylus struggles to negotiate the damage I inflicted.

The tissue-wrapped tooth was placed beneath my pillow when I went to bed that night.

Because the Tooth Fairy would come and leave me money in exchange for it.

She'd take it up to heaven, and use it to build the houses people live in after they die.

It would be used to build my mum's house, and she would know it was the same tooth she saw come through my gum a few years before.

By the front door, is where I imagined it to be, so she could reach up and touch it every time she came and went from her new home.

She'd never forget me, then.

Just as I would never forget her.

As long as I could play the record about nose-bumping and hair on end, I would always picture her in my mind, as she acted out her part right in front of me, as close as two people can be.

Come the morning, my tooth remained under my pillow.

For three nights, I left it there.

But nobody came.

On the third morning, I dropped the tooth in the bin.

And I stopped believing or trusting in anything after that.

31.

The cycling gloves and shoes improve my performance.

My fifteen to twenty minute stints are becoming easier, and I can maintain a steady thirty kilometers per hour.

In addition, I had to find a belt for my jeans, as I seem to have dropped an inch or two from my waist.

Strange growths are appearing on my legs. I think they might be muscles.

And my back doesn't hurt so much.

In fact, I have no pain. I'm pain-free. The bruises from my fall are now just pale yellow stains, like a dusting of pollen.

My hair requires cutting, but I can't be bothered.

Lisa used to do it for me, with a set of clippers. But when she left, she took them with her.

I'm not sure why. I've met Dave.

She took the scales, too, so I have no idea if my weight has altered since I visited the doctor.

That was six days ago.

A week tomorrow, and I'm due back at work.

It's the weekend, but there is no end to a week when you're doing what you enjoy.

Every day becomes the same, whether it begins with an S or not.

And S is the predominant letter when it comes to records in 1970, it seems.

Cat Stevens, Black Sabbath, Soft Machine, Spirit.

Dad is back to a record every week, approximately, so I go through 1970 in two days.

Vashti Bunyan, The Pretty Things, Van Der Graaf Generator.

Supertramp, Curtis Mayfield, T Rex, Hawkwind.

Some of it I know. Some of it I like. Some of it I don't. Still, I play every track on every side of every record.

It's a mixed year, that feels as though dad was mostly getting chart music, but keeping a toe dipped in the ditch marked 'underground'.

Another day passes me by.

A call from John Greene has me reaching for the volume dial.

"Sorry to have taken a while to get back to you, Dan."

"No problem. What's up?"

"I've been waiting on the MCPS-PRS."

"Any news?"

"Well, yes. And it's a bit strange, to be honest."

"From what I know about Tommy Histon, it was always going to be."

"Ha! Indeed. Well, you said your name was Danny Goods, right?"

"Yes. Why?"

"Your father... Was he a W Goods?"

"Bill. William. Yes."

"And did he live at 23B Market Street in Palmerton Chase at any point?"

"Yes. That was in the sixties, when he knew Tommy Histon."

"Then, it seems, your father is the registered holder of the copyright."

"But he's dead."

"It passes to his next of kin."

"Me?"

"Possibly, if that's where his estate went."

"Well, it all went to me and my brother and sisters."

"Then it could be split between all of you, if it wasn't stipulated."

"Buggerations."

"That's one word for it."

"I don't really understand. What does it mean, in terms of releasing the record?"

"It means you can do that, if your siblings are in agreement, I presume. It also means that all of the money it generates will come to you. So, any licencing of the tracks, any cover-versions, any radio play, and broadcast of any kind, will earn you a royalty."

"Blimey."

"There's more."

"Go on," I urge him.

"There's a back-payment to come from the acoustic demos. They're the same songs, so you have the ownership of those, too."

"How much?"

"I have no idea. They wouldn't tell me. You're going to have to get in touch yourself for that, and prove you are who you claim. And that you're the legal beneficiary."

I take down the number and contact name from John.

I suppose this means I should probably talk to my family for the first time in many years.

32.

'00470 - CA Quintet - Trip Thru Hell'.

A letter from dad, and a postcard are contained in the sleeve.

I read the postcard first: 'Greetings From Mexico! Hey man! Made it. Couldn't have done it without you and the Big Man. Life is great, so thank you! It was all worth it. Love and peace. MZ in the DMZ!'

'How are you, Dan?

Well, my record buying went a bit awry there, I think. There was no time, son. Between work and Trevor, I had my hands full. Half of my purchases were initiated by hearing a track on Radio One.

If me and your mum both liked it, I'd nip into Jemford Bridge or Drescombe and pick it up. That meant limiting any purchases to what they had in store at Woolworth's. Ideally in the cheap box.

And come the early part of 1971, we discovered Paula was pregnant with Beth (named for my Aunt Bet, obviously).

I was fine with doing that. The radio was a constant in the garage, as Goods Vehicles held its own. As a result, the records you've been playing were the soundtrack to that period in my life.

That's why I retain a fondness for them. Time and place again, son.

Paula and Trevor would spend plenty of time in the garage with Shorty and myself.

Your mum would answer the phone and help out with the paperwork and accounts, which was never my thing. It freed me up to do more repairs, and earn more money. We needed it.

Still, it wasn't quite enough. We'd overstretched ourselves on the house, and with another nipper on the way...

That was why I took a job for Ally Mac in late-August of 1971.

I was to take a van, a blue Commer, and drive up to Shropshire to pick up some recording equipment and a couple of jukeboxes.

No job for Ally was ever straightforward. And I should have sniffed a rat when it was decided that Darren would be coming with me, "to help out."

We set off early on the Saturday morning, thinking we could get up there, load up, get back to Norton Bassett and unload at the studio house, before calling at Ally's on the way home, all in one day.

The date is ingrained in my memory - August 28th.

Paula was heavily pregnant, so I was keen not to be away for too long.

The drive up was a bloody nightmare, as it was a Bank Holiday weekend. Everyone was heading to the Welsh coast, and those that weren't were trying to wriggle through to the English resorts in the northwest.

It drizzled stubbornly the whole way. We finally arrived at our destination near Whitchurch at two in the afternoon. I stayed in the van as Darren walked up to the farmhouse and knocked on the door.

A woman answered, and looked terrified at the large black man standing on her step. I honestly believe that she'd never seen a black man before. Winding down the window to listen, I heard Darren charm her with his silky voice, and ascertain that the man we wanted didn't live there.

He lived in a static caravan a couple of hundred yards off in a field.

So Darren headed over there, as I skipped out to follow, keen to stretch my legs after the journey.

The blast of a shotgun had us both diving face-down into the cow dung.

I'd never heard a shotgun close-up before. They're bloody loud, son!

Thankfully, it was fired up into the air, and we were both shaken, but otherwise unscathed.

"What the fuck...?" Darren shouted.

A slight, knot-muscled man, with longish fair hair, swept back from his tanned face, stood on the step watching us. The shotgun was draped over his arm, but still vaguely pointing in our direction.

He had stubble and narrow eyes. He looked like Clint Eastwood.

"He's only got one shot left," Darren whispered to me.

"That's one too many!" I hissed back.

"Split up. He can't shoot both of us with it that way."

"What?"

"Trust me, Bill, man."

We stood up, hands raised in surrender. I edged away from Darren, to my right, and put some distance between us.

"How'd you find me?" the man called out.

"We were given this address," Darren shouted back.

"Who by? Who betrayed me?"

I realised that he was an American. The second one I'd ever met. Were they all mad?

"Nobody betrayed you, as far as I know," Darren informed him, "we're here to pick up some gear, man. For Ally Mac."

"You're not Military Police?"

"No. We're from Brakeshire."

I nodded along that we absolutely were. No doubt about it.

"Well, why didn't you say? I could have fuckin' killed you both," the man said, and cocked the gun open, before spinning on his heel, and stepping into the caravan.

We approached cautiously. He was busy making coffee in a pot on the stove. I'd never seen coffee made that way before. In my experience, it was either instant, or from a machine in the coffee shops.

"You must be Matty Ziff," Darren said as we entered.

"That's me. Coffee?"

"Please," we both answered.

It smelt so good, Dan, the coffee in that caravan.

We seated ourselves outside, the caravan too small to comfortably accommodate us all, a canopy above the door keeping the drizzle off us.

"You got the Bill Of Goods?" Matty asked us.

Darren looked at me.

"No. There's no paperwork," I informed him.

"Ally told me to only hand over the merchandise when I saw a fuckin' Bill Of Goods," Matty growled, eyeing us cautiously.

"Oh, that's me!" I suddenly realised, "I'm Bill Goods."

"Your name's Bill Goods?" he asked.

I nodded.

And Matty Ziff burst out laughing so hard that he spat his coffee out in a mist all over the grass.

After that, and for years, I was often referred to as Bill Of Goods.

We sat with Matty Ziff for an hour or so, drinking coffee and sharing stories. He was in the US Air Force - helicopters, I think he said. Anyway, he'd been posted to

Germany for a time, which he'd loved. But then orders came through that he was being deployed to Vietnam.

Matty didn't want to go. It was as simple as that. He didn't agree with the war, and so ran.

He caught a fishing boat across to the Faroe Islands from Denmark, before another boat brought him to Scotland. Since then, he'd been hiding out for a year, always waiting for the military to catch up to him.

Time was getting on, so we headed over to a barn where the equipment was. There were two old Wurlitzer jukeboxes from the fifties, with domed tops and lights. And they were bloody heavy.

The three of us wrestled those things on to the Commer, the springs almost bottoming out once we'd slid them up planks into the back.

Soaked with both rain and sweat, we were done by about seven in the evening. We could be home that day after all, so long as we parked the van at my garage and dropped off in the morning.

We were in for a slow ride back, given the weight on the van. Darren would stay at mine, so we could get an early start on the Sunday.

I handed Matty an envelope that Ally Mac had asked me to give to him once the merchandise was secured.

He broke the seal and looked inside.

"My freedom," he told us.

I looked confused, so he pulled out a passport. "I'm going to go home, gentlemen. Well, actually, I'm going to go to Mexico. And my wife and daughter are going to meet me there. Wherever they are is home to me. We can begin again."

I nodded my comprehension, and smiled at him.

"She's ten months old, my girl. Ain't never seen her yet," he added, and smiled back at me.

There were tears in his eyes, Dan.

Children will do that to even the toughest men that I've known.

Of course, it made me think of Paula, and getting back as soon as possible.

We said our goodbyes, and went to leave.

The van had a flat tyre. And when I checked the spare, it was also flat. It was a new addition to Ally's fleet, but I should have checked it before setting off.

And it was too late to get another tyre, given the time of day. Back then, everything closed on a Sunday, and Monday was a holiday. I began to have a dreadful feeling in the pit of my stomach.

Beyond calling Paula from the farmhouse, there was nothing I could do that night. She was fine, she assured me.

So we settled down to a bottle of American whiskey with Matty Ziff.

Before the night was done, Darren and I had agreed to buy four and a half thousand old pennies from Matty. They'd been salvaged from the jukeboxes he dealt in. He'd let us have them for a tenner, modern money.

In addition, I'd committed to buying Ziff's vinyl record collection. It comprised of two hundred and four albums, and they were mine for one hundred and sixteen pounds.

Mindbogglingly, he'd carted his collection with him all the way from Germany. But there was no way he could take them on the next leg of his journey. And he needed the cash.

It was every penny we had saved, Dan. Our emergency fund. Your mum was going to kill me.

Darren agreed to buy his shotgun for a tenner, but Matty refused to part with his coffee pot.

We were drunk, but we knew what we were doing.

The plan was, he'd accompany us in the van in the morning, along with the records and pennies. Once back in Brakeshire, I'd pay him, and he'd go on his merry way to the next stage in his life.

Simple.

I barely slept a wink in the van that night. Darren snored for the entirety, and then claimed he hadn't slept at all.

Come the morning, we borrowed a car from the farm, and I took the punctured tyre into Whitchurch, where a local mechanic had agreed to do us a favour. For the price of a drink.

We finally hit the road at midday, the van threatening to break in half at every rut or pebble we encountered.

Day-trippers were on the road, but we snaked our way down towards Brakeshire, the traffic and weather thankfully lighter than on the previous day.

We happy-chatted the journey away, the radio blasting out songs and keeping us going, the three of us wedged on the seats in the front, the rear groaning all the way in protest.

For a while, the news on the radio didn't register with us.

I only heard it because we had to pull over and let the radiator cool down.

"Shhh!" I urged the other two as I tried to listen.

The old penny was to cease being legal tender as of September the first.

Now, I believe to this day that Matty Ziff had no idea. I honestly don't think he was trying to con us. He was simply getting rid of his worldly goods before heading out of the country.

In our foggy minds, we believed the next day, a Bank Holiday, to be the last of the month. So we were screwed.

It was only later that we all realised we actually had until the Tuesday.

By eight in the evening, I'd improvised a fan-belt from the elastic from Matty's underwear. Darren and I only had the clothes we wore. I topped up the radiator with rain water, and I'd managed to clean the fuel filter where it had clogged.

We were all exhausted and starving hungry. So, I limped to a pub, and parked up.

I called your mum with my last few pence of new money.

She was fine.

Ally Mac had been calling the house.

Between us, we had seventeen pence in cash.

Ah, but then Darren remembered that we actually had four and a half thousand old pennies. And they were still legal tender for another day.

Just because we couldn't bank them, didn't mean that we couldn't spend them.

We ate our fill and then some, son! We drank like fish.

The landlord knew he could bank the money on the Tuesday, so was happy for us to line his pockets.

I don't recall how much the bill was - the Bill Of Goods, as we termed it. We gave him all the pennies, anyway.

The three of us slept in the van. Well, barely. Darren snored all night, and again claimed that he hadn't had a wink of sleep.

With a head like a ringing bell, I nursed the van towards Brakeshire the next early morning, as Darren slept on, and Matty threw up out of the window.

We'd just crossed into Brakeshire when we ran out of fuel. The gauge was dodgy.

Knowing the area north of Jemford Bridge, I walked the three miles to a garage I knew through my business. It was closed, being a holiday.

I didn't have a penny on me. Not even an old one.

Now, picture me, son. I've been on the road for over two days, not changed, hardly slept, been shot at, had an appalling hangover, and was caked in dried out cow manure. My hands were covered in dry blood from working on the van with the minimal amount of tools, and I was in a panic about Paula.

I knocked the first door I came to, and a woman answered.

"May I please use your telephone?"

She looked me up and down as though I were an escaped murderer.

"Please," I urged, "my van broke down, and my wife is preg..."

"Bill?" she said.

"Yes," I confirmed, my eyes trying to focus on her.

"You haven't changed a bit," she exclaimed.

And I remembered then. She was a friend of my Aunt Bet's. And as a kid, twenty years before to the day, I'd fallen in a pond on a Bank Holiday day trip down to Drescombe.

I was covered in crap then, as well. I literally hadn't changed a bit. I'm not sure she'd have recognised me had I been normally dressed and turned out.

"I haven't been walking around like this for twenty years," I felt the need to clarify.

My dad drove up with the fuel.

From there, we went to Norton Bassett, and unloaded the recording gear. Then on to Ally Mac's, where the jukeboxes were manhandled into his house.

He wanted them down in the basement.

Our expressions alone ensured that he'd keep them on the ground floor.

From there, I drove back to Tredmouth to drop Darren off. He returned from his place with the money for the shotgun.

Finally, I headed home. Or, rather, I headed to the garage and opened the safe.

I took our life savings - all one hundred and sixteen pounds of it - and gave it to Matty in exchange for two hundred and four vinyl albums.

We'd agreed that he'd stay at mine for the night, before getting a train south in the morning.

So that's where we went. It was nine in the evening.

A one day job had taken three full days and two whole nights. I had to be back at the garage for six in the morning.

On arrival, I was confronted by the fact I had a baby daughter called Bethany.

She was two hours old, Dan, when I finally arrived back home.

The album in which this letter is contained, is the first of those albums I got from Ziff. It was the first I played that night.

The following two hundred and three were also his. Oh, and what a collection!

It was a treasure trove, Dan.

He'd brought half of them over from the States with him, including the CA Quintet LP. I'd discover Ultimate Spinach, The Fallen Angels, Velvet Underground, The Stooges and MC5. Then there's Fifty Foot Hose, Ruth White, Mecki Mark Men, all of which were on the Limelight label.

Thereafter, he'd been in Germany, and had discovered what would become known as Krautrock. He had the first two Can albums, Amon Düül, Popol Vuh and Kraftwerk.

At the time, I had no idea what a good deal I'd got from Matty. Only over the years did it begin to reveal itself, as the values went up and up.

I felt a guilt, that I owed him in some way. But how could I have ever contacted him? A postcard was the last contact I ever received, and I had no address for him.

But I've thought of him often over the years. I hope he went on to live a free and happy life with his wife and daughter.

Paula wasn't too angry about the records and life savings. She knew what they meant to me, and that Matty needed the cash. And I promised not to buy many records until the money was replenished.

And we never did pay Matty Ziff for our share of those old pennies. He was insistent on that.

The postcard arrived from Mexico about six months later. It's in the record sleeve, if you wish to see it.

Well, son, that's how I increased my record collection quite significantly in one fell swoop. And in the forty years since, I've never come across anything nearly as good.

And all because of a trip through hell.

Love, Dad.'

33.

Tracking the numbers, I can see dad was true to his word.

'00674 - T Rex - Electric Warrior' and '00675 - David Bowie - Hunky Dory', are the only two additions from 1971.

'Hunky Dory' is a brilliant record.

Not so long ago, a matter of weeks, I dismissed it because I didn't know it. I dismissed a lot of things because I didn't know them.

My family included.

"If it was any good, I'd know it," was my exact thought.

That version of myself is now repulsive to me.

Do I like every record that I've heard? No. The truth is, some left me a little cold.

But I've come to have respect for everyone making music and releasing it. Especially those that attempt to do something different.

I'm due to go back to work tomorrow.

A full month's salary was deposited into my bank account on Friday. Further, the music publishing people have photocopies of my birth certificate, along with the papers my sister, Beth, sent over. They included the birth certificates of my siblings, father, and an old bill showing that he lived at the address they have for him in 1964.

Just under ninety thousand is the amount due. It's broken down into how it was earned. Radio play, licencing, etcetera. A chunk of it came from Tommy's demos being used in a film.

It works out to twenty thousand each, plus change.

Moreover, it buys me time.

A year of freedom could be purchased with my share of the money.

It hits me just how much I've altered.

Time is the only thing I'm considering buying.

As dad wrote, 'time is the most precious commodity in life.'

It doesn't come cheap, but if, in the meantime, I can get 'Kimono For Kip' released on any kind of reasonable scale, I can prolong things.

After all, I'm not even ten percent of the way through the collection. Of the ninety-eight boxes, I'm half way through box nine.

It's taken me four weeks. Continue at that rate, and I can get through them all by Christmas. Or another nine months.

Babies are conceived and born in that time. Human ones, at least.

Lisa's baby.

God, do I still care about that?

Fair play to her. She got on with her life. She decided what she wanted, made a change, and went for it.

I can see now, that I've been sitting around for years, waiting for life to come to me.

Historically, everything has been provided for me. I am of that generation. I've never once voted, in any election or referendum.

Yet, I've sat and moaned about the result not going the way I wanted it to go.

Why? I have no right to complain.

I expected everyone else to go out and vote for the result I desired.

Deep down, perhaps I even do that deliberately, so I can't make the wrong choice. I cannot lose.

It also frees me up to attach myself to any side later on. Usually the side where the most attention and sympathy lie.

I don't make mistakes, and I'm never wrong. Because I never do anything that has consequences.

I believe in nothing, and have no passion for anything.

Not once in my life, have I had a clear vision of what I hope to achieve. Chemistry was something I picked, but never with any intention of doing anything with it. It was simply a way of prolonging the time before I had to get a job and be responsible.

And that's what worries me now. Am I doing the same? I can sit here for a year, pedalling the bike and eating healthily, and consuming dad's record collection.

But what then? I'm acquiring knowledge and getting fit, but to what end?

What do I want?

It was good, talking to my family. It's another positive step in the right direction.

They said that I should have the money; that they had the business and the house.

"No. Dad would have wanted us all to share it," I replied.

I shan't go back to work. I decide it in an instant.

But I've played out the sick-note card. So, I have to ante up, and play some different cards - a hand that will have consequences.

I may win, or I may lose. I may live to regret what I'm about to do.

Beyond that, I have no firm plan. It's all very short-term, living off the money I don't yet have through Tommy Histon's music. And that only generated ninety grand in fifty-five years.

It isn't going to be enough.

But I do have a safety net.

If I absolutely have to, I can always start selling these records.

As a last resort.

34.

'00721 - John Martyn - Solid Air'.

'Hey there, Dan.

You came to visit yesterday. It was good to see you and Lisa. You seem settled, son. I need you all to be that, as it makes it easier, knowing you are all okay.

I worry you're tired, though. But you're young enough to handle it, just as I was at your age.

You were a little tetchy when I mentioned about you two having children. I meant what I said, Dan. Do it while you have the energy. Don't leave it too late.

As we know, things can happen in life. Unseen events can come along very quickly, and rip your world apart.

Don't ever let it stop you living, Dan. Do that, and fear has beaten you.

After you left, Yvonne gave me a chiding for teasing you about it. But I wasn't really teasing.

Look, I was thirty-seven when you came along. And Paula became ill almost immediately. I wish we'd had you straight after Yvonne.

In fact, it has crossed my mind that, had we had you earlier, Paula may have been younger and fitter, and better able to fight against it.

Ah, but we can never know what might have been.

Don't listen to me. You have children whenever you feel ready, son. Or don't have children, if that's what you both want.

Lisa wants a baby, though, I think.

I saw her face when you snapped at me. She looked terribly sad, Dan.

Talk to her, pal. Ask her what she wants.

And then ask yourself what you want.

Just do that for me, please.

You may discover that you want different things, but at least, then, you'll be able to plan accordingly.

It was difficult knowing what I wanted in 1973, in terms of music. Most of the chart stuff did little for me, and it had been the case for a couple of years.

I was bored by many of the sixties bands that had endured, and didn't hear much to excite me in the new emerging bands.

As you will have seen and heard since my last letter, I did hold back on my vinyl buying after the Matty Ziff episode. And I did replenish every penny of our savings.

Your mum was wonderfully supportive of me and my music. I was so lucky to have met and married her.

She got me this John Martyn record for my thirtieth birthday. That alone is enough of a reason for me to love it.

Curtailing my collecting wasn't such a hardship, as I struggled to find records to buy.

Some of the more mainstream albums did appeal, such as Bowie, T Rex, Roxy Music and Mike Oldfield.

But the German scene was much more appealing to me, as I sought out the sounds Matty Ziff had introduced me to. Thus, you've played Neu!, Guru Guru, Grobschnitt, Embryo, Faust, Agitation Free, and others I can't think of off the top of my head.

A third side to my collecting was the enduring folk music. Old favourites such as Bert Jansch with 'Moonshine', John Renbourn with 'Lady And The Unicorn' and 'Faro Annie', Nick Drake's 'Pink Moon', and so on, were snapped up. My heart, I think, always lay in the folkier, softer side of things.

An album back in 1973 probably cost about as much as half a dozen pints in the pub. Or three packets of cigarettes.

The birthday card your mum got for me that year is tucked in the other side of the gatefold sleeve. It's been there for nearly forty years.

Have a read, pal, and I'll write again soon when Yvonne makes an appearance.

Love, Dad.'

'Happy Birthday My Darling Husband!

You are such a wonderfully generous man. I love you so much.

I had to get you a record for your birthday, because I know it is the thing you will value above anything else I might buy.

Hope I didn't mess up and get one you have! This is a new release, and I don't remember seeing it.

And, yes, I know you said you didn't want anything, and that the money would be better spent on a fancy new washing machine.

But you deserve it, and so much more.

Don't ever feel any guilt for the records you buy, my love. Never deprive yourself for us, Bill.

More than anything in the world, I want a happy husband. And I know you are. I have no doubt of your love for me.

You don't smoke, Bill, and you rarely drink very much. And, when you do, you have a drink at home with me. You work hard, and are as close to the perfect husband as I imagine has ever been.

You give me everything that I ask for, for myself and the kids. Thank you!

Your music is one of the reasons I fell in love with you in the first place. How many perfect hours have we spent with one another, listening to them, and loving them? And loving one another at the same time! More than I can count.

Records last for ever, not a day, or just a night. They will outlast you or I, Bill.

I wish I could give you every record ever made, my darling.

You deserve everything that your heart desires.

My love, all of it, is yours for all time.

Paula x.'

35.

'00722 - John Martyn - Solid Air'.

'Dear Dan,

I never had the heart to tell her I'd ordered the record, and had picked it up from Jemford Bridge the previous day!

Sometimes it's best to not share everything, I guess.

I know for certain there are many duplicates in my collection, mainly because of those car boot purchases that I forgot I already had! Or reissues of records I hadn't played in forty years, so had slipped my mind.

The memory goes as you get older, Dan. Trust me.

All of that said, I still bought them because I hadn't played it in forty or fifty years.

Thus, they served their purpose. They made me listen again.

And sometimes, I'd find little differences in the pressings.

In addition, albums that I wasn't keen on at the time, can often appeal later on in life. Taste changes.

So, I don't regret any of the duplicates. Not really.

They are, like everything else here, a continuation of the story.

Because in real life, we often do experience things more than once.

Unfortunately, I only got one of your mum.

There could never be another.

Oh, hey son, whilst I have you...

A few years ago, I was replacing a wheel on a car, and it made me think of a record as I span it on its axle.

The tyre was the playing surface, and the hub the label.

And as I sat looking at it, something dawned on me that had never occurred to me before.

We talk about the speed of a record being thirty-three and a third revolutions per minute. And that's true, but it doesn't really tell the tale.

If I pick a point on the rim, and another near the centre label, both points rotate that many times per minute.

To its outer edge, it has a radius of six inches. I sat and worked it out approximately, using pi and whatnot. You know more about that kind of thing than I ever did.

Anyway, to the best of my ability, I calculated that the outermost point on a record was moving at twenty-one inches per second.

The innermost point near the label, with a radius of two inches, was moving at seven inches per second.

Well, that blew my mind!

Moreover, the actual speed it was rotating altered at every point between those two. All of that had to be factored in to the manufacturing process, I presumed.

I am right, aren't I, son? I'm not missing something obvious here?

But the point at the edge of it all has so much further to travel.

It has such a long way to go.

Well, it made me think about life.

The world continues to turn at the speed it has always rotated. And we sit on it getting older.

Without really noticing, we slow down. We cover less distance.

To the eye, we're spinning at the speed we've always span at.

But we aren't. Not really. We take short-cuts and work smarter. We effectively do less, as energy wanes.

Yes, a tune is still delivered, and it will sound fine - no different to the rest of the record. But beneath it all, we're inexorably grinding to a halt.

I allowed my eye and mind to drift in to the centre of the wheel that day, Danny.

It went to the point where a stylus will never reach. Because life has no buffer cut into it, to stop us advancing past a defined limit.

We have no choice but to continue on our ever-decreasing course.

Do that, and the exact centre shall inevitably be reached. A radius of zero will be achieved.

At that moment, we shall cease to exist. No distance shall be travelled. No speed is reached. No energy is expended, so none is required.

It is death, son, that point on a record.

After Paula died, I had to become the centre of a wheel. And around my hub, the family rotated.

I fear most of all, that once I am gone, the pieces constituting my family will have no centre around which to revolve.

They will go off in different directions without that connection tethering them.

I hope I always allowed you plenty of slack, Dan, and I didn't pull on the tether too tightly.

If I did, I ask for your forgiveness, but it was hard for me to fully let you go.

You were as close as I could get to Paula.

But I know that, if you tie a dog up all the time, and keep it too close by your side, it'll run off the first chance it gets.

It's nature.

There was always too much pain associated with the family home. There was that lingering presence of your mother.

With hindsight, I should have moved. Moved house, and moved away. We should have started again, Dan.

But I couldn't leave it, the home I shared with her. I couldn't let go.

And by holding on so stubbornly, all I succeeded in doing was to drive you away.

I'm not perfect. I'm scratched and nicked and slightly warped by all I've experienced and endured in life.

Will you look out for your brother and sisters after I'm gone?

You must become the hub of the circle now. You're the strong one. You're like your mum.

Trevor worked in that garage with me for five years before we moved and downsized.

He was exposed to the asbestos in the building for all of that time. And even as a child, he'd come to work with me in the school holidays, and help out.

I fear for him, Danny.

The record finished a while ago. The needle has been buffering pointlessly for a long time now.

All of the tunes are played out.

But the world will continue to spin.

It's time for me to sign off.

Love, Dad.'

36.

They took it well, my work.

If anything, my decision to leave was met with relief.

I was also informed that cutbacks were going to have to be made, as printed papers continue to struggle.

As a result, my notice wasn't accepted.

Instead, I am allowed to be the first volunteer for redundancy.

That way, I get a pay-off.

It won't be that much, but a week for every one of the fifteen years I've wasted there buys me another few months of income.

Also, that way, if I can't get a job elsewhere, it'll make things easier regarding benefits, as I won't have voluntarily quit my job.

I know I should be somewhat worried about the future, but I'm not. All I feel is a massive sense of relief.

Even the redundancy discovery made it feel as though it was meant to be.

An allen key tightens a bolt. Record shelving begins to appear. It feels good to be building something.

I messed up the first one, and had to take it apart and begin again. I didn't read the instructions. Arrogance.

Turn, turn, turn, whether it be bolts or the pedals on the bike, I keep turning things. Just as I turn things over in my mind.

And, as it was for my father, the records continue spinning all the while.

The world keeps on turning with me. Because it always does. No decision I make will change that.

Life goes on.

My parents were in love.

I never really knew or understood that until now. Sure, dad would tell me that he loved my mum. But it was always, to me, just something people said.

Similarly, he would tell me that he loved me. He has done in his letters. But they washed over me, those words.

They did so because I have never known adult love. As a result, I'm incapable of understanding or truly feeling it.

Perhaps, too, I've never loved myself. If I can't do that, then I have to be incapable of loving anything or anyone else, don't I?

Was it because of mum dying?

I think so.

Love died with her.

Even though I have very few vivid recollections of her, I am aware that she was my whole world. In her was the purest love, and once it was snatched away, nothing was ever likely to compare.

Her going slammed closed a door I've never dared open since.

I always kept a barrier in place, so I might never be hurt like that again.

I didn't love Lisa. Not in the way my dad loved my mum.

And I don't believe she really loved me.

We'd say it, in that way people do; quickly, like a routine, and with an equally rapid reciprocation.

Where mum supported dad in his record buying, Lisa and I were resentful of one another's interests and ambitions.

My dad had a room in our home, where he would store and listen to his LPs. And my mother supported and enabled that.

Lisa and I had huge arguments about the spare room being full of boxes.

Ah, I'm being too harsh. I did nothing with those boxes for over six years, and I never once thought of supporting Lisa in her dream - to have a child.

I think that was all she really wanted from life.

I'm happy for her. I love her just enough to be happy for her.

She was braver than I was. She made the change.

Me? I would have continued on as we were, making each other miserable most of the time.

Better the devil you know. Play it safe. Keep carrying on. Don't rock the boat, baby, don't tip the boat over.

How many copies of Tommy Histon's 'Kimono For Kip' will I need to sell to prop myself up?

Firstly, I need to clear my debt. I can do that, just about, with my share of his back catalogue, leaving me the redundancy money to live off. It will last me approximately four months. Five, if I really scrimp.

Any royalties earned from the release will be split four ways, but will take a while to materialise.

The records, though, are legally mine to do with as I please.

Twelve thousand pounds for the copy of the Histon LP keeps flashing in my mind.

I picture it there, and count the zeros. I imagine it in my bank account, and know I can pay my rent and bills, and live off it for a year when combined with the other money I have coming.

Twelve thousand is the offer John Greene called me with from one of his THAS members. Twelve grand for that played copy of the album.

What would dad do?

He always appeared to be so safe and conservative when it came to such matters. He talked about work and responsibility. He preached about being debt free.

Yet, he spent their life savings on two hundred and four albums.

Those records have now appreciated to be worth, I would guess, several thousand.

And I know the answer to all of my financial worries sits in the boxes he left me, but I can't think of letting them go.

Tack, tack, tack goes the backboard on the shelving.

"It'll contain them, and stop the records being pushed out when you file them away."

My father taught me that.

37.

'00740 - The Wailers - Burnin'.'

'Hello mate.

Me again!

If there is one record I think of as being synonymous with Darren, it is this one.

We were spending more and more time together, whether it be through work or outside of that.

All through the year, Darren had been playing Bob Marley's music non-stop. 'Get Up, Stand Up' had been released just before the album came out, as I remember things, and was on rotation.

His DJ career was on the up, as reggae music became more popular, and I'd spend many Friday and Saturday nights driving the van to a club or hall somewhere in Brakeshire.

Baz Baxter used him a lot, and he had a residency at his BB Nightclub most weeknights.

But, if live music was on the menu at the weekends, Darren was free to accept other gigs. I helped him do that.

We'd load up the old blue Commer I had on an almost permanent basis, and head out to some wedding or birthday party somewhere.

Darren would pay me, and we'd get a couple of free drinks each as part of the deal. I was always driving, so would only ever have one.

From arrival at a venue, we could have everything up and running inside twenty minutes, we had it down to such a fine art.

And we had some wonderful laughs, Dan, he and I. Yes, I did it for the money, but I'd have done it for free, had Darren needed me to.

Around 1973, I started to notice a second-hand trade picking up on records.

A stall appeared in Tredmouth market, down on River Road. It was run by a man called Roger.

Darren got a lot of his ska and reggae import singles from there. Roger would drive to Birmingham or Liverpool, and pick them up from the parts of those cities that weren't the most salubrious.

Despite being born in Jamaica, Darren had lived in England since the age of twelve. He was a few years older than me, so was nearly forty when I was thirty. He always wore a white woolly hat, even in the heat of summer.

"Why do you wear that hat in the summer, Darren?" I'd ask.

And he'd just smile me away and wink knowingly.

As well as the reggae music, he'd spin the hits of the day, along with a few oldies. It all rather depended on the audience. Thus, a few cases of pop and rock singles went in the back of the van.

He'd get some looks, would Darren, being a huge black man DJing in working men's clubs.

It was better if they believed that I was the DJ, and he was helping out.

"Open box three," he'd whisper to me, once he'd gauged his audience.

I'd rummage around in the dark behind the console, and locate the case numbered accordingly.

It was the one holding his rock'n'roll singles.

"It's an Elvis crowd, Bill man. Throw in a bit of Mud and Mott The Hoople, and we'll have them bopped out and too tired for any trouble."

I'd walk out into the audience to check the sound, or to fetch a drink for us both. All I could see amidst the smoke and lights, was a nodding white woolly hat, and a big white-toothed grin that was impossible to not smile back at.

Sure enough, come the end of the night, all of the snarling men at the beginning would come up and thank Darren for the brilliant music.

He nearly always got another booking as a result.

To be honest, nobody was going to give us any trouble in the more cosmopolitan Tredmouth, where Darren was well known. He was also known to be an associate of Baz Baxter and Ally Mac, which further insured him.

The only really bad night we ever had was over in Millby.

When I was young, Millby was a fairly insignificant place. It was a little dot in the middle of the county. In fact, it was two little dots, being split into Upper and Lower, both of which were not much more than villages.

During three decades from the end of the war, it began to very quickly develop. Being centrally located, and with good road and rail networks, businesses moved in, as did a workforce. There was a huge influx of people from far and wide, and housing was thrown up quickly and cheaply to accommodate them all.

As a result, it struggled for an identity. It was a fractured place, where old and new didn't really mingle.

Come the late-fifties, I would cycle over, if you recall, to buy my records. The population there, unlike in Palmerton Chase, warranted a decent record shop. But there was always an atmosphere that I can't really explain.

It's changed in the time you've known it, but those changes didn't occur until the eighties. By then, the money was rolling in, and it has since become one of the best places to live in the entire county.

Well, in November of 1973, that wasn't the case.

Each time we unloaded something from the van, I'd lock the doors. It slowed us down, and we were still sound-checking when the people began to arrive.

Shorty was on duty at home, protecting Paula and the kids, so wasn't with us.

It was a fundraiser for the local football club, and the crowd split into huddles, depending on where they came from. Upper Millby here. Lower Millby there. Oaklea Estate to the right. Riverside Estate to the left.

It was a grim time, son. Wages had been frozen by the government, and strikes seemed to be being called everywhere. The IRA were detonating bombs all over the place, and electricity use was set to be limited to a three-day week because of a fuel crisis.

Even the motorway speed limit had been reduced to sixty from seventy, angering many. And seeing how Millby was the distribution hub of the county, it angered people there more than elsewhere.

Yes, it was an angry room we played that night.

Darren had no idea what to play. The skinhead contingent would be up for the reggae, but that would piss off many of the others. There were northern soul boys and girls, and mods, and then a majority who would want the glam pop hits of the day.

Most worryingly, there was a group of old school rockers who would want box three and some pub rock.

"What do we play?" I asked Darren.

He shook his white-hatted head. "When all else fails, Bill man, you play what you know best."

Thus, 'Get Up, Stand Up' was the first track to blast out of the speakers.

It was only as the second track began, that I realised Darren had put the album on, and not the single.

He stood there, smiling and nodding his head in time, and played the whole album. Both sides.

And when it was finished, he flipped it over and played it again.

"Can't please all the people all the time, Bill, so you may as well please yourself. That's my motto in life!"

The audience was seething, but no trouble erupted.

Darren switched to some current glam chart fodder.

Everyone was so relieved, that nobody complained. They got on with it, and danced for the next three hours to whatever they got served.

I shook my head at Darren as we stood there watching them all bobbing up and down in the lights from the disco. To David Cassidy, The Osmonds and The Carpenters.

"Give them a common enemy, Bill man. Now they hate me so much, they forgot about hating each other."

His grin lit my face up.

It was the last time I'd see his smile exactly like that.

He lost his front tooth, Dan, after we loaded the van.

I got away comparatively lightly, with cuts and bruises and a cracked rib.

Even then, I think the cracked rib came from Darren throwing me into the van for my own safety, with the words, "look after my hat, Bill!"

A bike chain opened Darren's body up in a vicious strip, and a knuckle-duster did for his tooth.

He hospitalised three of them, and inflicted at least as much damage on each of them as we suffered between us.

It went to court, and Darren was acquitted. It was clear to all that it was self-defence. I gave evidence on his behalf.

Prior to that, I drove us to a hospital.

All the way there, he kept asking if his hat was safe.

"Yes, Darren. It's in the back of the van. Now let me try and focus on the road."

Stitches were applied, and they patched us up. Darren would need a false tooth.

At six in the morning, we arrived back in Palmerton Chase.

The following morning, a Monday, Paula gave birth to Yvonne, and The Wailers 'Burnin'' was the soundtrack to that, too.

Paula requested it. We were sick of hearing it, to be honest! But we couldn't refuse her.

Darren lived with us for two weeks while his body healed.

And I discovered he had a little pocket stitched into that white hat of his. Inside it was where he kept his stash of marijuana.

I'm sorry the record is a little scratched, Dan. It has been played many times over that weekend, and since.

It was Darren's, but he gave it to me after Yvonne arrived.

And I've cherished it ever since.

Love, Dad.

PS - the blood on the sleeve is Darren's, not mine!'

38.

Why did it dwindle, I wonder?

Was music not very good in the mid-seventies?

Dad bought less than fifty albums over the next three years. It's barely one a month.

He was what age? Thirty to thirty-three.

I did the same.

We hit thirty, and something alters. Priorities shift, and we settle for what we have. Or what we are. We become a bit closed.

Is that the time when we think we know it all, as we get nostalgic for all that has been, rather than what is to come?

Are all of our best days behind us at a third of a century?

In addition, in dad's case, he had three kids and a business to run. I reason that he probably didn't have the time or money to indulge himself too much.

He did buy some great records, though. Eno being a highlight, as well as the more ambient German artists that came out of the harder early-seventies scene.

But there was a conservatism that had crept in. The artists, with few exceptions, were known to him, as they'd been releasing in other guises for a decade.

I've spent much of my listening time reading up on music generally, as well as specifically with regard to individual records and artists.

Popular music, and mass-produced records that contained it, really took off after the Second World War. So, music itself is hitting its thirties by the period I've reached in this voyage.

Come 1976, and it is a thirty-something.

However, I also know that the staid state of affairs is about to be smashed to smithereens by punk.

Dad always said that punk came along right when it was required. Just as Elvis did twenty years previously.

"It was the kick up the backside that moved things on," was his way of phrasing it, "even if it was a step or two backwards in some ways."

I smile at that, and wonder if it isn't what I'm doing with my life. A step back to get ahead.

Dad was quite a few years younger than I am now when punk happened. He always had a fondness for it. I do know that.

"It made me feel like I could actually be in a band," he'd tell me. "Before punk, I was always in awe of the musicianship and songwriting, I suppose."

"Were you ever in a band, dad?" I asked.

"No. It never happened. Too much other stuff going on."

I remember him being a little sad when he told me that.

But he soon snapped out of it.

I was in a group, and he was chuffed to bits about it.

He was so supportive. I'd forgotten about that.

It was in 1995, when I was fifteen. Britpop was massive, and myself and a few school mates decided to form a band.

Every Sunday afternoon and Thursday night, Goods Vehicles became our rehearsal space. Dad got us a basic four-track tape recording system, and some microphones. He knew how to mic up the drums.

We were impressed by that, my mates and I.

Just as we were impressed by his offer to sponsor us through the business, and hook us up with someone he knew through Darren, who might be able to help us get a record made.

"A CD," I corrected him, and he smiled.

I don't remember what we called ourselves.

But I do know that we never actually completed a proper song. We played at it, and spent most of the time planning rather than doing.

I dabbled around on the keyboard, making patterns that, to me, sounded like hits. Bits of hits, anyway.

"You have to practice, son," dad would say, until it sounded like nagging.

And after about two months of meeting twice a week and making plans, we just stopped.

The gear was left in the garage, and the keyboard and amp became things on which other things could be stored. The drummer took his drums home with him.

The Brake Down Vehicles. That was the name of the band.

It broke down. And it never got repaired.

Just like everything else in my life.

39.

'00801 - The Stranglers - Rattus Norvegicus'.

'How are you, Dan?

I hope you're happy on whatever day this is for you.

I am. Today was a good day. All four of you, my children, were here.

I've been thinking about the sixties. Not the decade, but the age.

It should have been our time; mine and Paula's. Hitting sixty was the marker we always discussed.

We'd travel a bit. Not far. But we planned on trips to the seaside, or walks in the grounds of National Trust properties.

Financially, we'd be fine. Not rich in cash terms, but rich in other ways. Because, when you hit sixty, there isn't much you need or want.

We'd have served our time. Sixty was the time to reap the rewards.

And so it should have been.

Live for today. It's a track somewhere on an album, but I forget who recorded it. I expect I could look it up in half a second on the internet. That's the way of things now.

The computer thing - a Tablet, is it? - that you all chipped in to get me was very thoughtful. I shall try to use it more, to look up such things, I promise.

But I can sing the song in my head, and that's enough for me, son. Beyond that, I don't require the details.

I was never one for studying the sleeves and liner-notes. Who played which instrument on each track was never the point. It was always about the music, and the moment that it represented.

Our retirement years, and the time we had earmarked for one another exclusively, were never reached. But you know that.

Don't even bank on tomorrow, son. If it's important to you, do it today. Now. This instant.

That is the most vital snippet of advice I can ever give you.

Appreciate every single thing you have right now. Change what's wrong. Do more of what's right.

Where are we? April of 1977.

I'm chuckling away to myself here, and I've not written about the events yet.

Punk had taken over the country, it seemed. In the space of less than a year, everything that was established was torn to shreds.

And I loved it. Music was beginning to bore me. It was all very complex and technical. It lacked the energy that had always attracted me since the rock'n'roll of the fifties.

Baz saw the potential of punk early, and opened his doors to all of the odd looking youngsters that were a part of the scene. For it was a youth movement. I was a granddad at thirty-three or thirty-four.

But I did embrace it. Paula began cutting my hair short, and spiking the top with some gel. And I took to wearing t-shirts and jeans more. It was my very sedate little punky rebellion!

When The Sex Pistols came along, and others my age were smashing their televisions the December before, I sat there laughing at it all. It was brilliant, I thought. And Paula agreed.

Of all of the bands, though, The Stranglers were my favourite. It may have been because they weren't really punk. At least, their music wasn't.

To me, they were more of a prog rock or pub rock band at that stage. And they always struck me as being very clever.

Baz Baxter's 'It's Tred Dad!' boutique was renamed 'Brake Up!'. Gone were the Afghan coats and kipper ties. In were the garments of the era.

Darren and I blasted out punk and reggae at the relaunch, until the police came and asked us to turn it down a bit.

Paula was meeting up with Ally Mac at our house a couple of days a week, and sketching out clothing designs for Baz to have manufactured. She made some good money from doing that.

It went into our retirement fund, and ultimately helped pay for your university degree!

Ha! I bet you never knew that. Punk helped pay for your education!

Anyway, amidst all of it, Darren decided to learn to drive. That isn't strictly true. Darren could already drive.

He decided to take his driving test, and get himself a car.

"Bill man. I need to be more mobile," was his way of telling me that.

I gave him a look.

He explained. "I'm going to buy a car, man. And I've found one that I fell in love with!"

"Well, that's great."

"Will you come and take a look? Check it out for mechanical soundness, and all that."

"Of course I will. Where is it?"

"Oakburn."

"What is it?"

"A car."

"No, what make is it?"

"How should I know? I like the shape of it, though. It's beautiful."

"Okay. How much is it?"

"Fifty quid."

That worried me a bit.

"Have you had a look at it?"

"Yes. From the bus."

"From the bus?"

"Yes, man! I saw it out the window of the bus. It had a piece of card in the front saying 'For Sale - fifty quid', and it looked like a nice shape. The kind of shape I could get on with."

"Have you had a bit too much weed?"

"No. Why?"

"Oh, no reason. Apart from you sound like Tommy Histon. When do you want to go?"

"Now, if you can. Before someone else snaps it up. It's a bargain, Bill."

It was a quiet Tuesday afternoon, and Aunt Bet was helping out with the phone. Paula had her hands full with your brother and sisters.

"Oh, and Bill?"

"Yes Darren."

"Can you teach me how to drive so I can pass my test?"

"Erm, yes."

"Thanks, man."

"How will we get it back?" I asked.

"You could take the trailer, I thought."

"Okay."

"I mean, it probably wouldn't make it all the way back here, anyway."

"Hang on," I said, as he went to walk out, "it's only thirty-five miles. Why would it not make that?"

"It needs a bit of work, Bill."

"How much work?"

"A bit. It's a nice shape, man. I love the shape of it."

"Is it the shape it's meant to be?"

"Roughly."

"And you don't know what car it is?"

"It's my car, I hope."

"But it needs some work, you said?"

"Some."

"Okay."

"Good job I know a good car mechanic, eh, Bill man?"

"That was a stroke of luck," I said sarcastically.

We hitched up the trailer, and got in the van.

I'd recently picked up 'Rattus Norvegicus', and had taped it, so that was what we listened to on our journey over.

Darren hated the album.

All the way, I tried to imagine what car Darren would be attracted to. I kept picturing something American, with wings and chrome, and a big roaring engine. Knowing him, it would be something he'd seen as a Matchbox car, and had then spotted the real thing.

What I never imagined was the cream-coloured 1968 Fiat 500L I was confronted with.

It was probably the very last car I could have thought of.

And it was a mess, Dan. Fifty quid seemed a bit of a rip-off, to be frank.

But Darren was absolutely smitten.

"I can get you something better, Darren," I proposed.

"Better than this?" he replied with incredulity.

"Okay, then I can get you something bigger."

"No, man. This is my dream car."

"Get a grip on yourself, Darren."

He shook his head. It was pointless to try to dissuade him. He was having the car.

"It's going to need a lot of work," I pointed out, as I looked it over, "where has it been stored, at the bottom of the lake in Norton quarry?"

"How long will it take to get it roadworthy?" was all Darren was bothered about.

"I have no idea, to be honest. Quite a while, I should think, by the looks of it," I answered, pushing my hand through the rust-hole in the floor on the passenger side.

He could barely fit through the door, and he banged his head on the roof every time he drove over a cat's-eye, but he was adamant that he wanted it.

In the end, I got it him for forty-five quid. And the seller walked away with a big grin at that.

But his grin was like a frown next to the sheer delight on Darren's face.

I whipped the cassette out of the van, and inserted it into the player that had been fitted in the Fiat.

It played.

It was the only thing on the car that actually worked.

Almost. The eject function was broken.

And I left the Stranglers tape in there for the six months it took to get the car roadworthy.

Once it was, and Darren had finally passed his test on the fifth attempt, I left it in there for another three months, and rewired it so the play function was permanently on.

He adored that car. It was completely impractical for all he wanted a car to do, of course, and was constantly needing work, but he simply refused to part with it.

He called it Peaches.

The night Paula died, he drove over to the house in his Fiat 500L, and sat with me all night. You were asleep in your room, Dan. And you'd awake to the very worst of days.

"It wasn't just the shape, Bill," he whispered to me as we sat waiting for Paula to die.

"What?" I said, not understanding.

"The car, man. My dream car."

"What about it?" I asked, turning to him.

"It wasn't just the shape that attracted me to Peaches."

"No, well, it's a fetching shade of light brown. There's no denying that, Darren."

"It's cream, Bill," he said, in absolute seriousness.

We both started giggling. It felt so wrong, giggling like that, like a couple of children, as the morphine removed all of the character from Paula.

"So," I managed eventually, "aside from the shape and colour, what is it about that Fiat, Darren?"

"Three things, to be honest with you, man. First up, it couldn't really go fast enough to do any damage and get me in trouble."

"Agreed," I agreed.

"Second, no self-respecting police officer was ever going to pull me over in that car."

"There's probably a lot of truth in that," I concurred.

"And third, and most important, it meant I could spend lots of time with you, as we fixed it up and you taught me how to drive."

I dropped my eyes from his self-consciously, and smiled down at my hands as he sat by my side.

He added, "and because it's a piece of shit, Bill, we get to do that on a regular basis for ever. You'll always be needed, you see?"

I briefly laughed.

His hand found mine.

So warm.

I remember the heat and life emanating from him, Dan. And strength. I felt such strength in him.

"She's gone, Bill," he whispered.

I looked up.

And Paula, your perfect mother, was dead.

Love, Dad.'

40.

I understand.

There's so much that I now understand.

I know why dad wanted me to buy a Fiat 500 when they were relaunched ten or twelve years back.

I know why he always said the music I listened to and liked was, "a ringer for such-and-such."

He was right.

"If you like that, you should listen to so-and-so," he'd attempt to guide and steer me, but I never allowed it.

That was old. That was the past. Fuck that.

Besides, I always interpreted it as him trying to say his music was better. But he wasn't saying that at all. He was simply trying to establish some common ground; something on which we could gel and have a conversation.

He was looking for something to bring us closer together.

But I always pushed him away.

Not just him.

I pushed everyone away. I always have.

There is no equivalent of Darren in my life - the man who will sit with you as you lose the most precious thing in the world. A man who will hold your hand, and tell you that you are needed.

A man who will make you laugh, just as the worst of all things comes to pass.

My father was at least twice the man that I am.

I knew Darren.

He was my godfather.

How old would he have been? Fifty, approximately, when mum died.

So not that old.

They'd laugh, dad and Darren, when I was ten or twelve or fifteen. They'd sit and share memories, and they'd cackle away like kids, drinking their beer and playing their cruddy old records.

So I'd sit and watch my television in my room, and try to block them out, those two old men with their stupid stories, and my 'Uncle' Darren, with his daft hat and embarrassing car.

My godfather.

They'd joke about it all in front of me.

Oh, how they'd laugh!

Darren died a couple of years before dad.

He rang me, my father, his voice heavy, the words cumbersome as he struggled to hold his emotion in check.

"I'm sorry," I managed to say back, keen to get him off the line, something unmemorable on the television that I was missing.

It was truncated, my response. The full version would have been, "I'm sorry, but I don't really care."

We fell out about it, my father and I. It was because of the funeral.

I didn't want to go, so I made an excuse - something about a course at work - and copped out.

He didn't speak to me for a while after that.

He also asked if I could arrange an obituary in the Tredmouth paper.

"I'll see what I can do," I lied.

And promptly forgot all about it.

I am such a first-rate cunt.

And so I act.

Changing the record from '00802 - The Damned - Damned Damned Damned' to '00803 - Thin Lizzy - Jailbreak', I begin to tap on my screen.

I write down everything I know about Darren Smith, from his early life in Jamaica, to his moving to Brakeshire. I research him on-line, and get the name of the Youth Centre he ran for nearly forty years in Tredmouth.

There's a group for former members. I join it, and begin asking questions. Many knew my father as well as my godfather. Nobody has a bad word to say.

Emails are dropped to a few local bands who are still active, asking for their memories of the man.

Two get back to me almost immediately. One is a big name. Both state that they would never have had a chance were it not for Darren Smith, and his encouragement and facilities.

The respondent, the singer, tells me how he doubts he'd be alive were it not for my 'Uncle' Darren.

"Mind me quoting you?" I ask.

"Not at all. It's true," comes the reply.

I effortlessly bang out a fifteen-hundred word piece under the banner 'Local Heroes', and email it to my old boss.

By the time I get to switching from ELO's 'Out Of The Blue' to The Sex Pistols 'Never Mind The Bollocks', I have a reply telling me that my piece on Darren is a great idea.

They will pay me by the word. How about making it a monthly thing in the media section? Anything else of local interest that might work?

I mention Tommy Histon's time in Brakeshire, Baz Baxter and Ally Mac.

And the deal is sealed.

It isn't much, the rate per word, but I don't need much.

For Darren and my dad, I'd have done it for free.

In fact, I'd have paid to get it in there.

41.

'00844 - Kate Bush - The Kick Inside'.

'Hello Dan.

Paula adored this album. I think if she were here, and I asked her, she'd pick this as her favourite of all time.

I cherish it because of her.

It was in January of 1978 that she was first diagnosed with breast cancer. They caught it early, Dan, and we didn't hang around once we knew.

In fact, there was no real time to think about it. That was true for me, at least. I'm sure your mum had far too much time to sit around and dwell on matters.

Life changed for all of us in the space of twenty minutes on a Wednesday afternoon.

You think you're cruising, son. All the hard work is done, and life is good. We had three kids, aged eight, six and four. And Shorty, of course, who I'd had for eleven years.

We owned our own home, and business was steady enough to give us a good lifestyle. There was nothing, so far as I can recall, that we wanted but didn't have.

And then along comes cancer.

I had no doubt Paula would beat it.

Indeed, we planned around that, booking a holiday in Tinbury Head for the July of that year. Six months for us to remove it from our lives.

Nothing anyone can tell you will prepare you for chemotherapy.

I have no shame in admitting that I doubted my ability to see it all through, and I wasn't the one getting the treatments.

Darren, my family, and especially Aunt Bet, kept me going.

Darren helped out in the garage, and they took it in turns to look after the kids when I went to the hospital with Paula, or was otherwise occupied.

They all played their part in helping your mother, and our marriage, survive. It is thanks to them that you exist, Dan, and that isn't an overstatement.

Because survive she did.

So many evenings, as she lay on the sofa waiting for the next bout of sickness, were spent listening to this album.

She'd ask for it, and I'd play DJ. Despite everything, it would make her smile. 'The Man With The Child In His Eyes' was the track that always got her, and she'd gaze at me when it played.

I'd sit on the floor, a bucket permanently to hand, and stroke whatever part of her body didn't hurt too badly that day. I'd get a cold beer to drink, and roll the can gently over her brow to cool her head and stop her sweating.

And she'd smile and relax, and hum along to the songs.

She never once threw up when this album was on.

It became a joke between us. If she felt nauseous, I'd stick Kate Bush on, and she'd settle down.

I asked her once, "why do you like that 'Child In His Eyes' song so much?"

I thought it might have something to do with me.

"You don't want to know, Bill love," she gently replied.

"I do. I want to know everything about you."

"No, it wouldn't be fair on you."

"Whatever it is, it's the past. It's your past, and I want to know. Even if it relates to someone else."

"It makes me think of a choice I once had to make," she said with a smile.

I was happy to leave it at that, but she added, "it is about you indirectly. But it's about someone else, too. I made the right choice, Bill. That's all you really need to know."

We all have our secrets, Dan. There are some things that are better left untold.

But I wish she'd told me that day. I wish I hadn't found out in the way I did.

Your mum had very little to do with her parents.

She didn't have siblings, which is why she was so adamant we would have more than one child. You were the cherry on the top of that particular cake, Dan!

Anyway, her parents came to the funeral, accompanied by a man I presumed to be her uncle, or a close family friend.

Her mother and father made the day about them. Whilst I agreed with their sentiment that no parent should have to mourn a child, they were, in my opinion, and putting it mildly, a little selfish.

What about the four young children who had lost their mother? And, yes, what about me? I was thirty-nine, Dan. And it felt like the world was at an end.

"If she'd married Michael, none of this would have happened!" her mother rasped at me on the day of the funeral, as we arrived at the pub for a drink.

"I think she'd have still got cancer," I pointed out, but not nastily. I wanted the day to pass without any hitches.

"Oh, probably. Though there are no guarantees, of course. But if she'd married Mike, she'd have been in London, where he would have picked it up sooner, and treated it properly the first time!"

I bit my lip and said nothing.

"This is Mike," her mother said by way of introducing me to the man in their company. "He's a doctor."

I took the hand he offered.

"Sorry for the loss," he said to me.

I've thought about those words for years now.

The loss.

Not 'sorry for your loss'. The loss.

A shared grief for all. It implied that his loss was just as great as anyone else's.

"Thank you," I replied rather flatly.

I knew there was something amiss in his words, but wasn't capable of processing it properly.

And as I looked at him, his hand still grasped in mine, I saw the playfulness in his eyes. I saw the child in them.

Paula's mother began sobbing loudly, as we stood awkwardly around a table outside.

It was a beautiful warm day, son. Your mum would have loved to have been there.

"Oh, Mike," she wailed, "why didn't she accept you sixteen years ago!"

Her husband tried to calm her. "Now, now, Dorothy, it's too late for all that now. What's done is done. No sense in upsetting yourself."

"But if she'd married Mike, we wouldn't be in this awful place, and none of this would have happened!"

Ally Mac appeared by my side, Darren alongside him.

Ally was wearing a black shoulder-padded sequined top, with a long black skirt that stopped just short of a pair of black suede pixie boots. It was the eighties.

His lace-covered index finger pointed at all three individually, as though he were counting.

The fourth time he pointed, it was at the gates.

"Fuck off," he said quietly and calmly. He might have been asking them if they needed a drink.

"I beg your pardon!" Dorothy screeched.

Still pointing at the exit, Ally repeated, a little louder, "fuck off. Now."

The two men were already edging away, Paula's father tugging on Dorothy's arm.

Darren stood by with his arms folded.

That was the last I ever saw of any of them. They never wanted to know you children after that day.

Ally took me to one side.

"They're talking shit," he growled.

"Are they, though?"

"She told me all about it, Paula did. It was one day when we were designing a dress for Baz. And she told me all about Michael fucking MD, and the marriage her parents had planned for her.

"He's fifteen years older than her. I had the prick checked out. She liked him as a friend. A family friend. She'd share her troubles with him, and he'd listen. They were close for a while, back when she was deciding things. Back in the sixties.

"But not like that. At least, she didn't feel like that. He probably did, the fucking chancer. I don't doubt he tried it on. And she was flattered. He was a rich doctor. Naval background. But she didn't love him. She loved you. She told me that."

"When? When was that, Ally?"

"In the sixties..."

"No, when did she tell you?"

"Oh, I don't know. When she had cancer the first time, I think."

I got it. She was ill. Of course she'd be thinking of the choices and decisions that led her to where she was. And of course she'd be thinking of the doctor she might have married, and the difference it could have made.

"Thanks, Ally."

"It's Alisha now," he winked at me, "but Ally still works."

When I listen to the song, Dan, I can't understand it. Yes, there's the man with the child in his eyes, and that's obviously the doctor. But is the love it mentions referring to that man, or another?

Because it mentions nobody knowing about her love, and her family did know about Michael. It was me they didn't know about.

Then there's the line about the sea, and he was in the Navy.

Paula wasn't around for me to ask, and I don't know the answers.

But I do know that I can't dislike this LP, despite all it holds.

You didn't come to the pub. Aunt Bet took you home with her after the service. We decided it would be for the best.

I agonised over the decision, Dan, but I'm glad you weren't around for it. It was better you spent time with Aunt Bet.

That day was the last time you ever saw her. Within a week, she was also dead.

Twelve days after we buried Paula, I went to her funeral in the same cemetery.

You had to spend a lot of time with my sisters, if you recall. As did Beth and Yvonne. Trevor tended to stay with me, being a teenager and more independent.

Trev told me years later that he felt the need to stay close because he was worried about what I might do if I was alone.

Imagine the burden on a boy barely in his teens. I've always felt such a... I don't know the right word, son. You'd know which word to use.

I suppose it's a guilt I feel. Trevor didn't ever get to have a real childhood from that day on.

The day of Aunt Bet's funeral, I arrived home in the afternoon. Trev was at school, and the house was empty.

I called for Shorty, as he could always lift my spirits.

But he didn't come.

I found him lying in his bed.

And when I bent and put my hand on his head, I knew that he, too, was dead.

Within nine months, both of my parents had joined them.

It felt personal. It felt like I was being punished for something, but I had no idea what.

It was then that I became angry. I channelled the anger, and used it to survive. It was all I could do. It was my way of carrying on.

Work was my outlet. Beneath a car, or with my head under a bonnet, I could, to some extent, hide.

Cars were something I could fix, and make well again. I could bring them back to life.

That was the man you knew from that day forward.

No wonder you moved away and stayed away.

I don't blame you. It's what I wanted to do, if I'm honest.

Catch you soon, pal.

Love, Dad x

PS - I realise I've jumped ahead of the narrative there, son, but I wanted to get it out of the way. One cancer led to the other. It was the same cancer. And it came back. They are inseparable. But, the reality was, as a family, we had over four more wonderful years together. Not to mention a new addition! And that's what I want to focus on. The positives. It's time to focus on the positives.'

42.

I do have patchy memories of the funeral. One is very vivid, as I was led forward by dad, my hand in his. I copied him as we both scooped up a handful of dirt and tossed it down on the coffin.

It's the sound of the impact that remains with me. A hollow thud. It made me think she wasn't inside the box at all.

Once again, sound carries the recollection.

I drown out the sound in my head with The Undertones, Skids, Tubeway Army, Squeeze, Nick Lowe, Blondie and The Ramones.

The remainder of 1978 and early-1979 fly by, as dad is back to buying at least one album a week. The Knack, Generation X, Magazine, Buzzcocks, Sparks and The Clash.

ABBA. One for mum, I guess.

Can and Kraftwerk are still present. The Fall, Lene Lovich, Siouxsie And The Banshees, Motörhead and The Jam.

The Grease soundtrack. Mum. No question.

Bob Marley and Burning Spear keep the flame burning on the projectile thrown by Darren all those years before.

For three days solid, I listen to them all with a sense of anticipation that I am about to enter the world.

Dad was right. He was right to get mum's death and funeral out of the way. It's been hanging over this since the outset. And, even though it hasn't yet happened in the timeline, the truth is, it took place thirty-seven years ago.

Was it the most important event in my life? Yes.

I know it was the same for dad, but for different reasons.

His was a sense of loss stemming primarily from knowing what he was missing.

Mine comes from never knowing what might have been.

I can only blindly speculate on how my life might have panned out had she been around. For I inherently know things would have been different.

I would be different.

A conversation with Lisa comes to mind. It took place not long before she left. It was summer. Mid-June.

"It's worse for you," I told her.

"Why? Your mum died when you were two. I can't imagine anything worse than that."

"But I never knew her. Not really. Your mum left. She chose to leave you. My mum had no choice."

It depressed Lisa, that observation. But I stand by it. It's true.

She fired back with, "then why are you the one with all the abandonment issues?"

"I'm not," I snarled at her, getting defensive.

"You are! And you're so risk averse!"

"I'm not," I said lightly, trying to laugh it off as ridiculous.

"You are. There's something fatalistic about you. It's as if you don't see the point in doing anything for the long term. There's no commitment."

"Crap. I do plenty," I countered, but I knew in my heart that she was right.

"You never do anything with your life, Dan. You play it safe. You've done one job at one place all your life. You've lived at two addresses in thirty-seven years of existence. You've rarely ever left Brakeshire. And you're terrified of having children."

"No I'm not. And it's three addresses."

"Two. Staying at my old flat for eighteen months doesn't count."

"My bank statements were sent there. So, yes it does."

"It's not really the point, Dan. You never do anything! Look at the room upstairs! Five years that crap has sat there untouched."

"That's what spare rooms are for. Besides, I've got plans for those records."

"Plans? What plans? You've never had a plan in your life. Well, if you do, it's a plan that best ensures nothing ever happens."

We'd both had a couple of glasses of wine. It usually ended up in an argument.

"When the time's right..." I tried to protest, knowing anything I might say would be bullshit.

"We're running out of time!"

"What do you mean?" I asked, even though I knew perfectly well where she was headed.

"We're not getting any younger, are we? I'll be forty next year."

"The back end of next year. It's nearly two years away."

"A year and a half. We're running out of time, Dan."

"You are. I'm not."

"What does that mean?"

"You know what it means."

"No I don't. Tell me."

"It's just your hormones screaming, Lisa. Time of the month, and all that. You'll be okay in a few days."

She shook her head and huffed.

We both sat staring at something on the television. I had no idea what we were watching. It was shit. But it was better than having the conversation we were.

After a while, Lisa quietly said, "we need to either come together, or..."

"Or what?"

"Or not."

"What does that mean?"

"Nothing."

I never thought she'd leave. I honestly believed that it was an empty threat.

Do nothing was my plan. Do nothing, and she'd get over it.

The following day, the Saturday, we had some of her friends round for a barbecue. They were her friends. I had none of my own. Her friends were my friends.

Nikki was there. I liked Nikki. She was a fun girl, all bubbly personality, fake tan and long blonde hair. Lisa knew her through her work.

The weatherman lied. It drizzled in the afternoon.

Still, I cooked the sausages and burgers, the grill beneath the lean-to at the rear of the house. It was where we ordinarily stored the bins.

Lisa was inside, busy making a salad and putting nibbles in bowls.

I'd already had a few beers, even though the party had barely begun. A night on the sofa hadn't improved anything from the previous day. I was busting for a pee, but didn't want to go inside.

Nikki came out for a smoke. She'd arrived early to help.

Before she could spark up, I asked her if she'd keep an eye on things while I nipped round the side of the lean-to to relieve myself.

She nodded.

So that's what I did.

She was suddenly behind me. Reaching round me, she grasped hold of my dick.

"Save you having to wash your hands," she whispered in my ear.

I've always had a bit of a problem going in public, but I needed to so badly that it didn't hinder me.

Things began to respond, even in mid-flow.

When I was finished, she shook it, tugging firmly. Too firmly. There was no doubt she could feel the swelling.

"All done," she purred, after a few extra unnecessary pumps of her hand.

"Thanks," was all I could think to say.

It was a struggle to get things tucked back away, the front of my trousers bulging as a result.

I turned around, and Lisa was stood behind Nikki, holding a tray of baking potatoes she'd cooked in the microwave. I was to keep them warm on the grill, and crisp up the skins a bit.

Nikki went to take the tray from her.

"Wash your hands, Nikki, please, before you handle the goods," was all Lisa said before walking back to the house.

I drank and drank that day, but couldn't seem to get drunk. I found myself watching Nikki at every opportunity, before guiltily locating Lisa.

She never seemed to notice. It was as if she didn't care.

That night, as I bedded down on the sofa, Lisa popped her head round the door.

"Night, then," she said.

"Nothing happened," I told her.

"No, it never does."

She stood there, regarding me. I could see the sadness carved into her face.

Sad Lisa.

"We'll sort things out in the morning," she finally sighed.

"There's nothing to sort out, Lisa."

"I was talking about the mess in here," she replied, and went up to bed.

The following day was Father's Day, so we drove over to Lisa's dad's house for midday. The journey was silent, except for the radio playing a selection of father related tunes, such as Harry Chapin.

Just as Harry worked out that his boy was just like him, Lisa said, "watch yourself with Nikki, Dan."

"There's nothing to watch."

"I've known her sort all my life."

"There's nothing to worry about."

"Oh, I'm not worried," she calmly stated, as we pulled up at her father's.

Bryan, her dad, had remarried twenty years before. He was a perpetually happy man, whose personality showed via the red clownishness of his cheeks, pulled around by his dancing grey eyebrows.

In the pub that day, he jovially asked when we were going to make him a grandfather.

"When we're ready," Lisa responded with a modicum of forced optimism.

And I sat there smiling it all away, as, in my mind, I imagined having sex with Nikki.

When Lisa left seven months on, I called Nikki after a few days. I reasoned that a few days was an acceptable period to wait for such things, seeing how I was the one abandoned.

She fobbed me off with something about being Lisa's friend.

I presume she told Lisa that I'd asked her out for a drink.

"I tried to warn you, Dan," she said when she popped round for a few of her things, including the clippers and scales.

"What's that?" I asked nonchalantly.

"About Nikki. I tried to tell you."

"What about her?" I shrugged.

"She only wants what other people have, Dan. She never wanted you. She wanted to take something from me."

"Well, I never wanted her, so it doesn't matter."

"Right," she smiled, "take care of yourself."

And she was gone.

43.

'00918 - The Specials - The Specials'.

'Hello Dan, my boy!

Well, we finally got a family holiday in October of 1979. A year and a bit late.

As luck had it, the weather was good that month, and it was mostly dry and sunny, with temperatures around seventy.

We took the kids out of school for a week, and set off to Tinbury Head on the Sunday morning. It was an easy drive down to the coast, it being out of season.

Darren offered to look after Shorty, and keep things ticking over at the garage, in part exchange for all the work I'd done on Peaches.

He and Trevor had developed a shared love for the Two-Tone music that was coming out. They'd both taken to wearing porkpie hats and calling one another rude boy.

Rather than the tent we usually spent our holidays suffering in, we splashed out on a B&B. Life was good again, and we felt as if we all deserved a little pampering.

We ate out every night, and the landlady was happy to rustle us up sandwiches for lunch.

Paula was free of the cancer, and feeling better than she had done in two years. Trev, Beth and Yvonne were all doing great at school, and were popular, well-adjusted children, despite the scare of the year before.

Knowing The Specials debut LP was due out that week, I wanted to get a copy for Trev. To that end, I asked the landlady, Mrs Pearce, if there was a record shop in town. She was a lovely woman of around sixty, who could talk for England, and often got her words wrong.

"Oh, yes, love. Woolies have a deportment upstairs, and the electronical shop carry a few bits and pieces. And then there's Head Music over on Sandy Lane, just up the hill a bit from the seafront. It all depends what you're after, I suppose. My Clarrie, god rest his soul, loved his classicals, he did. He could tell you all of the composings, and who played what on what. Very knowledgabubble about that was my Clarrie."

"Sorry for your loss, Mrs Pearce."

"Thanks, love. It's been a while now, but I continue to feel his presents. I'm sure his aurora still lingers! At night, you know, and I shouldn't say this really, I sometimes feel him get into bed alongstride me. I'll just be noodling off, when I'll feel his arm come around me, and his hand... Well, between us, and not for the little ones plugholes, I'll feel his hand on my bosom! I know, I know, I tell myself, it isn't real, it is all in your imaging. The mind is a powerful thing, Bill, if you don't mind me calling you that and being familial?"

"Not at all," I said, edging towards the door.

"Here, I'll tell you something else. On numerical occasions, I've come home from bingo of a Wednesday evening, and walked into the front room, like you do, and I've heard a funny noise going ba-bump, ba-bump, ba-bump. Things that go ba-bump in the night, I suppose you might term it!"

"Well, I won't keep you any longer..." I tried to excuse myself.

"Hold your horsehairs, don't you want to know the finishing?"

"Oh, sorry, I thought you were..."

"Manifestoons! Goolies! That ba-bumping was a record turning on that there steroid system. Round and round it would be a-going, having played all the way through. Well, I'd shake my head and tut, and lift the stylius off the record and click the button to stop it rotatoring. 'If you can put it on, you can very well take it off again!' I'd say to him, but not in a bad-tempered way. He was always doing that, was my Clarrie, leaving the stylius on the record like that!"

"Perhaps a guest..."

"Ghost! Yes, I believe that it is his ghost, his spiritation, as you might term it. It's the remainderer of him. It's quite fluttering, really, to think he can't bear to move on and leave me."

"It's very sweet."

"Still, I think if those old vinile records of his weren't here, he might be able to get a shift on."

"A shift on?" I asked.

"He'd be able to get to where he needs to be a bit quicker, love."

"Oh, I see. Well, it's possible," I said, humouring her.

"Here, you don't want them, do you?"

"What sort of music is it?"

"Classicals, like I said. That was his thing. Always going on about red seals and Deutschie telephones, he was. There are about a hundred of them in the bottom of the cupboard there. You'd be doing me a favour, you would, taking them."

That was how I came to have a hundred classical records, Dan, which you're about to come to.

It took me a long time to play them, as they weren't really my thing. They're all in lovely condition, as old Mr Pearce must have cherished them. Each is marked in pencil on the rear with his initials, 'CP'.

Paula knew a little about classical music, so one day over Christmas, she put on Tchaikovsky's 'Swan Lake', and

Debussy's 'Clair de Lune'. And I fell in love with music all over again, son.

It's funny how things come to us only when we're ready. I'd always dismissed the pre-rock era, apart from the blues, as being an irrelevance. But at thirty-six, I was open to it. It seemed to fit with where I was in my life. Most importantly, it would help me deal with what was to come.

I shall always be in Mrs Pearce's debt for those records.

"Let me pay you for them, please?" I implored her.

"No!" she protested, holding her palms up to me, "just promise me that you'll take good care of them."

"I promise. Why don't you want to keep them, Mrs Pearce? Won't Clarrie be upset?" I asked, not quite believing that I was joining in with her delusions.

"Oh, I'm sure he will, love. But not as upset as I'll be if they stay in this house!"

"Why?"

She lowered her voice to a whisper, so that I had to lean in to hear her. "Between you and me, love, and this is off the record, if you'll pardon the punt. I'm up on the third floor, see. That's where I sleep, for as long as my legs can manage the stairs. The second floor is for the guests. Well, by the time he's put a record on, got all the way up there, undressed his self, got into bed, draped that arm over me and locationed my bosom... Well, let us just say that the side of the record is about at its climactic, and I'm nowhere near mine!"

"Erm..."

"So, off he goes, like a ghost in the night, back down the stairs to turn the vinile over, and we go through all that again. Over and over. Time after time. All I ever feel is his hand on my bosom, and his breath on my neck! I wake up to silence, with just the ramparts of his contact left on my body. So, you can probably see why I want rid of them!"

"Understood."

"I knew you would, love," she said, and patted my hand.

I finally escaped, and walked into Tinbury Head, where I bought The Specials LP on vinyl and cassette, the latter being for Trevor.

That evening, I gave Trev the tape, and he was so happy, Dan. I picked up sticks of rock for the girls so they wouldn't feel left out.

Paula and I laughed for hours at dear Mrs Pearce and her story. She thought it was so sweet.

We all went to see Grease at the cinema that same night. Mrs Pearce came with us as a treat and a thank you.

Paula had wanted to see it for a year or more, since it had come out, but circumstances had prevented that. She loved it.

And later, once the kids were asleep, I lay spooned into the back of her, my breaths hot on her neck, and her 'remaindering bosom' cupped in my hand.

"Bill?"

"Yes, Paula."

"I'm pregnant."

She said she could feel me grinning in the dark - she could hear my cheeks stretching, as the flat of my hand dropped to her stomach.

We drove back on the Sunday, Trev's tape blasting out all the way home on repeat, the car laden down with a hundred and one new albums to explore.

It felt like the dawning of a new era, as we all sang our heads off.

Love, Dad x.'

44.

'01048 - Martha And The Muffins - Metro Music'.

'Hello Dan, in more ways than one!

Well, it took me twenty-two years to accumulate a thousand records, thanks in part to Mrs Pearce, Ally Mac and Matty Ziff. Between them, they accounted for about half of them.

It works out to not far off a record a week.

I hope you played all of the classical albums. I'm not so keen on the operatic records generally, but thankfully Clarrie was a strings man like myself.

Over the next twenty-two years, I would add perhaps four or five thousand.

As the eighties progressed, so compact discs came to be the format on which most people wanted their music. I was never too enamoured with them.

They were handy, for sure, but I didn't like the size and plasticity of them. Just as I didn't like the plasticity of the sound.

And they were expensive, Dan, when they first came out.

But, I must concede, it was largely due to CDs that I added to my vinyl collection so rapidly.

By the end of the eighties, car boot and jumble sales were rich pickings for vinyl collectors like myself. That went on for a decade and more, until the internet enabled everyone to become a record dealer in their spare time.

Oh, but I took advantage of the period, and filled in many gaps, as well as discovering music I wasn't even aware of.

The problem with buying records in that way, is there are very few moments and memories I can link to those purchases. I was buying so many so often, that they all kind of merged.

It would sometimes sadden me to see a forlorn batch of albums or singles in a cardboard box in a field. Surely, at some time, those records held precious life moments.

What could have happened to make people give their memories away like that?

Still, their loss was my gain, as I'd rise early on a Sunday morning, and drive to car boot sales all over the county and beyond.

Do you remember coming with me, Dan, when you were small? You'd pick through a box of toys, and choose a car or action figure for yourself.

Quite often, thanks to your keen eyesight and height, you'd spot a box of records beneath a table, and alert me to it.

"Records, daddy!" you'd exclaim, and point to where they lay.

"Good lad. I'm sure you can smell them," I'd smile down at you.

More often than not, they were tatty and not my thing, but we discovered a few absolute treasures over the years! We were a good team, son.

And we'd grab a bacon or sausage sandwich from the burger vans that were usually present. We'd sniff them out, as well.

The glorious aroma of onions and bacon sizzling on a griddle, and merging with the grass and fresh air, on a bright Sunday morning! I'm not sure I've ever known a better smell than that.

I've always associated it with you. Even recently, if I catch that scent in my nostrils, I picture you toddling around a field.

The early starts did for you in the end, I think. As you matured, so you didn't want to head out at seven-thirty on a Sunday morning. I didn't blame you.

But I enjoyed it, so continued by myself, or with Darren.

Do you remember one May morning in about 1990, when it suddenly began teeming down with rain?

The ground was already sodden, and hundreds of cars were parked on the field over by the racecourse near Wrenbrook.

Vinyl in hand, we sprinted for the car. So did everybody else. It was a mess, with people slipping and sliding all over the place.

A hundred cars began snaking and skidding, churning up the mud, and getting bogged down on the slope.

Old Darren was so proud, as his lightweight Fiat, with you, me and the engine weighing down the back end, weaved through them all, and made it out of there without so much as a wheel-spin.

He did love Peaches.

Things moved on, as I said, and come the internet age, clicking buy on a website became the way of it. There was no adventure associated with the hunt in the main.

The thrill of the chase was lost. Every record one could ever think of owning was there and available. It was simply a matter of having enough money to buy it.

A chance discovery at a car boot sale was absent. The buzz of buying a record, and getting home to play it, was somewhat gone. There were very few bargains to be had.

Yes, there were disappointments in doing that, as albums failed to live up to expectation. But there was always a thrill.

The trouble with the internet, I think, is that you only really search for things you already know.

Ah, I'm jumping ahead of myself again.

Martha And The Muffins was the album I picked up in late-February of 1980. I can tell you that I got it at Boots the chemist in Drescombe. Can you believe Boots used to have a record department? I think it cost three ninety-nine, but I could be wrong.

'Metro Music' was due out and expected in February. You weren't. You were due in the first week of April.

You were always eager to reach the next stage when you were little.

The half-term day began with Yvonne, who was six, falling off the bike she was trying to learn to ride. Trev let go of the saddle, and she rolled down the hill without stabilisers for the first time.

Unfortunately, she wasn't ready to negotiate the bend at the bottom, so went straight on into a wall.

She cracked her collarbone, and cut her face. The cuts upset her more than the broken bone, I think.

I got a call and came home early to look after Trev and Beth, while Paula took her to the hospital.

She was back within a couple of hours, her arm elevated in a sling, but no other treatment required. She was always a pernickety little thing, though, and was as upset by her inability to ride the bike as anything else.

And she did like being the centre of attention.

Nothing's changed, eh? Don't tell her I said that!

I was playing an album the following afternoon, having taken a day off work to help out. Paula was heavily pregnant with you, remember.

"Bill, Yvonne wants you to play a different record!" Paula called to me.

Ambling through from my room, I asked, "which one do you want to hear, Vonny?"

"The one about the baker," she said sulkily.

Well, I was flummoxed. The baker?

Seeing my confused expression, she added, "the one we heard in the car on Saturday!"

I went through the journey in my head. We'd gone for a short drive down to Drescombe in the afternoon, and stretched our legs in the little valley at the base of the hills. We'd planned on walking the lake, but the weather had come in suddenly, so we'd postponed. It was only ten miles each way, so perhaps time for a dozen songs.

For the life of me, I couldn't remember any of them.

Yvonne began to get frustrated.

"You know it, daddy! It was on the radio!"

I racked my brain. Baker?

"Ah, 'Baker Street', by Gerry Rafferty!"

It was only a couple of years old, so it had to be that.

I put the album on.

"Is this it?"

She shook her head miserably, her poor shoulder beginning to hurt far worse than it had when she thought I knew the track.

"How does it go?" I asked her.

She made a noise that sounded like nothing at all musical. Paula and I looked at one another, and shook our heads.

I asked Trev and Beth, but they had even less of a clue as to what she was on about.

"Uncle Darren will know!" Yvonne snapped, stamping her foot. All that did was make her arm hurt even more.

I rang Darren.

"Easy, man!" was his boast.

"Go on."

"Boney M, 'Ma Baker'. Has to be."

"Shit, I haven't got that."

"I have."

"Really?" I said, somewhat surprised.

"Yes. Why?"

"No reason."

"I'll be there in half an hour."

"In your car?"

"Good point. I'll hopefully be there in an hour."

Yes, I did kind of remember hearing it in the car on Saturday, I thought.

We managed to get Yvonne somewhat settled by the knowledge Darren was on his way with the song she 'needed' to hear.

Fifty minutes later, he walked in clutching the single. Yvonne's face lit up.

On it went.

Yvonne's face was thunderous. It wasn't the song.

Shit. She was getting really upset. Her bottom lip was her most protrudent feature.

"Small Faces, 'Song Of A Baker'," was all I could think of.

She was screaming, the tears running off her cheeks.

"It won't be that," Paula said. She, too, was beginning to get worked up by it all. Yvonne was inconsolable.

"Bread?" Darren threw in.

We just looked at him.

"Can you sing it, Vonny?" Darren asked. He was the most laid-back man I ever knew, but even he was getting jittery.

She tried again. Given the state she'd got herself in, it was worse than before.

We collectively shrugged.

Shit.

Darren started calling out random words, "pie, pastry, crust, cake, sandwich, roll, loaf, muffin, bap, cob..."

Yvonne stared at him, her tears checked.

She nodded.

"Which one, Vonny? Which one?" Darren desperately cried.

"Cob."

"We stopped off at the baker's," I remembered, "and picked up a crusty cob loaf, Paula! Do you remember? Tell me you remember!"

"Yes! Yes! I got one for your mum, as well. So what was the song playing when I went in to get them?" she asked me.

"No idea!"

"Shit."

"Was it about a cob, the song?" Darren asked her.

Yvonne nodded, and added in a whisper, "and a muffin."

I clarified with, "so, it's a song about a muffin and a cob?"

"Kind of. It's not really about a muffin," Yvonne mumbled.

"But what is it?" Paula asked of anyone and everyone, as the crying threatened to recommence.

We all looked blankly horrified at one another.

And right then, Darren began to emit his deep hearty laugh.

He leaned forward with his hands on his thighs, and sank to the floor on his knees. His head was back, his mouth wide.

"Brilliant!" was all he could breathlessly say.

Shorty jogged over to make sure he was okay.

"What is it, Darren?" Paula asked, a pleading for knowledge in her voice.

"Absolutely brilliant!"

"But what is it?" I screamed at him. "Pull yourself together, man!"

"Martha And The Muffins!" he managed.

And he began to sing, kneeling on our floor.

"A cob each, far away in time!"

"That's it, Uncle Darren!" Yvonne announced triumphantly.

"'Echo Beach'," I elucidated, "I actually said that. When you asked if you should get a loaf for mum, I said, 'yes, get us a cob each'."

"Play it, Bill, for god's sake, just play it!" Paula added.

"I haven't got it," I confessed.

"Me neither," Darren added, as I looked to him to save us all.

Yvonne began to wind herself up again.

"Just go and get it, Bill, you have to go and get it!" Paula insisted.

We took Peaches down to Drescombe, and found the LP in Boots.

Thirty-five minutes was the total time it took us. We didn't even park. Darren waited with the engine running. We were both too afraid that, if he turned it off, it might not start again.

Your mum's waters broke five minutes after we left.

She waited. It was the longest thirty minutes of her life, she later claimed.

We rushed through the door, and all hell had broken loose.

Paula was, literally and without overstatement, holding you in.

Yvonne was screaming again. Beth, typically, cleaning up the mess. Trev was as pale as a ghost, and pacing the kitchen in his porkpie hat, with his hands over his ears. Shorty was howling at all the commotion.

You were five weeks early.

Your mum rarely swore, Dan, but as we entered, she wailed, "play the fucking record, Bill! Just play that fucking song!"

So that's what I did. Then I rang for an ambulance.

Darren picked Paula up in his arms, and carried her through to the bedroom.

By the time I arrived, he was holding you in his hands, the cord still attached.

"What do I do, Bill?" he asked, utterly calm.

"Slap its back!" I said, because I'd seen it on the television.

Lifting your ankles, your head resting on his leg, he gently patted your back.

And you began to cry.

Crying was good.

You had to be breathing to be crying.

"Let me see," Paula asked of Darren.

He held you to her, such a gentle man in spite of his size.

"Hello!" your mum said to you, "aren't you the little miracle?"

She looked over at me, a content smile now evident, in place of the anguish.

"Bill, come and say hello to Danny," she invited.

It was decided that night in Tinbury Head, after we went to the cinema.

"If it's a girl, Bill, can we call her Sandra, and if it's a boy, can he be Danny? Is that okay?"

"That's fine by me," I told her.

So, my son, 'Echo Beach', or 'A Cob Each' was the song playing at the exact moment you entered the world.

Blame your sister for that.

Darren was the first person to ever hold you post-womb.

And you were named for a character in Grease.

Love, Dad x.'

45.

It's time to move.

In every sense, that statement's true.

What happened to me? Where did that young lad who was always in a hurry go? At what point did I stop exploring and looking for what was next?

I've sat here for weeks now, pumping the pedals on a bike that goes nowhere.

Well, it's time to get back in the saddle.

My landlord is a man named Chris Baxter. I wound up living here because dad knew a man in Tredmouth who owned property. It was why the rent was always kept low. It was a favour stemming from an old friendship between my father and a man named Baz Baxter.

I call Chris.

"Chris, hi, it's Danny Goods."

"Oh, hello Danny. Been a while."

"It has."

"What's up?"

"Nothing. Well, something. I'm ringing to give you a month's notice. I'm sorry if it gives you a problem."

"It's no problem. Not with the rent you've been paying!" He laughs.

I join in, and add, "I can't believe I've been living here for so many years, to be honest."

"There's nothing wrong with the house, is there? Are you okay?"

I think about the answer to his question before replying, "actually, yes, I'm fine, thanks. You know Lisa moved out last year, and I'm ready for a change. That's all it really is."

"Fair enough. What kind of change?" He sounds genuinely interested.

"I want somewhere a bit smaller and a bit cheaper. I quit my job, Chris, and I'm ready to start something else."

"Again, fair enough. I appreciate you letting me know. Where are you thinking of going? Back to Palmerton Chase?"

"No, I don't think so. But I do want out of the city. I fancy somewhere quieter and more in the country."

"You know, if it's of any interest to you, I've got a place. It's a nice little cottage, about five miles southwest of Millby."

"Erm, that might work. How much?"

"We can work something out. Look, our fathers go back a ways, and it's important, that history. My old man always said, 'Goods are good people'. What are you doing tomorrow afternoon?"

"Nothing I can't postpone."

"Why don't I swing by, and we'll nip over and have a look at the place. It's just been fixed up and painted, so it's ready to go. Every day it stands empty is costing me money, and I know I can rent out the place you're in, no bother."

"And charge more rent!" I toss in.

"And that. We could grab a drink, if you like, and chat things through."

"Yeah, I'd love that. Thank you, Chris."

"I'll see you tomorrow, about three. Okay?"

"Okay."

I wasn't expecting any of that. This time yesterday, it hadn't even occurred to me to move. I think the seed was planted by half clearing the spare room.

As the floor became more and more exposed, a grid of box-marked flattened carpet was revealed.

For the first time in six years, I can fully open the door.

Because I could, I ran the vacuum cleaner round, and watched those flattened thirteen inch squares begin to rise and disappear.

In not much time, all trace of them shall be removed.

It's a good thing, that clearing of the decks.

Polyvinyl chloride, I think to myself as I file records on the shelves, ensuring I maintain my father's sequencing. PVC. My chemistry degree isn't entirely wasted.

Phthalates are probably added to the mix. I don't know that for sure, but it's a safe bet.

How strange that I'm doing this knowing I'll be moving soon. All of these will require repacking. It's why I keep the empty boxes.

The Cure, Joy Division, Dead Kennedys, The Clash.

The Feelies, XTC, The Soft Boys and Ultravox.

They, and many others, take me through 1980. I was alive when all of these were brought home and played. Some of the tracks - quite a few - are familiar. But is that from then, or from later, via the radio?

There's a box set by Eddie Cochran, taking me back almost to the beginning, and the first gig he ever attended.

Dad was a loyal friend. He stayed true, but always moved on. He embraced change, but never forgot the past.

46.

'01099 - Not The Nine O'Clock News - Not The Nine O'Clock News'.

'Hello Danny!

Do you remember this one?

You were generally a happy child. But you were teething, and having a terrible time of it.

The only thing that would settle you down, we noticed, was when 'Not The Nine O'Clock News' came on the television. Even though you couldn't really understand it, you'd lie there with your eyes fixed on the screen smiling away to yourself.

It was the most bizarre thing.

When they did 'Gob On You' you sat there chuckling away like a lunatic.

So I went out and got the album for you. It was your first record, I suppose.

But it didn't have the same effect. It was their antics on the screen, and their wonderfully expressive faces that captivated you, we came to realise.

It still makes me smile as I sit here and listen to it, though.

We're rapidly reaching a point in time of which you will have recollection.

Playing through my life in this way, I think I've laughed far more than I've been sad. That has to be a good thing. Moreover, I hope it implies I was a good man, for the most part. And that I lived a good life.

I can't really tell you what first led to my passion for vinyl records. Of all the things in the world one can get obsessed about, I wonder why that one called to me? I've never collected anything else. It has always been vinyl, right up to the end of my life.

One love, I suppose.

It was the same when it came to Paula.

Yes, there was the very dear Helen Clancy. But my sentiments towards her are born from guilt, and from, I think, hurting her.

Paula was, hand on heart, the one for me. I knew it when she was the mysterious Madeleine Michey.

Do you know, I've only slept with four women in my entire life? Five, if you count Madeleine separately.

God, listen to me. You don't want to know about that. It's bad enough having to think about your parents doing it!

When Paula died, I still felt loyal to her. Nobody compared.

Looking back, I think I should have tried harder to embrace another life. Thirty-nine wasn't so old. I could have begun again. It was, given the average lifespan, not quite the half way stage.

Okay, so I shan't make the average, but I still had thirty years ahead of me.

And, had I had a reason not to go to work at every opportunity, I wouldn't have spent so much time in the old garage, breathing the asbestos and hearing it fall from the ceiling in rusty drops that would, on occasion, land with a plop in my tea.

We all have choices, Dan.

I chose my path. And I opted for the past rather than any future.

Did I begin buying so many LPs after Paula died because I was looking for something? Did it plug a gap?

Was I desperately attempting to unearth new memories in those records, that would oust the old ones, but without me ever having to let go of the past?

I don't know the answers.

What I am sure of, is music gave me a reason to continue.

Hunting vinyl got me out and about, and forced me to interact with others.

If I am sad as I sit here writing, it's not for anything that has been and gone. It's for all I shall miss.

That's you children, and my grandchildren, primarily. I will not be here to see you all mature and succeed.

But, and as I said at the outset, I want to be honest; I also have a heavy heart because of all of the records that shall be released, and I will not get to hear.

It breaks my heart to think Robyn Hitchcock, for example, will release albums I won't get to enjoy.

If some latter day equivalent of punk were to come along, and shake things up in the way it did thirty-five years ago, I'd like to be here to witness the revolution.

But life does go on.

And, ultimately, it's an irrelevance to Robyn Hitchcock, or anyone else, whether I'm here to buy his record or not.

Enough people will.

Your mum told me, when she knew there was no way back - she told me to carry on, and to look for happiness elsewhere.

She asked me to do it for the sake of you children.

I think I should have tried harder for you.

Would you have liked a mother figure in your life, Danny?

Why am I asking that now? It's far too late.

I should have asked you thirty years ago. Just as I should have asked how you were, and listened to your answer.

I'm sorry, Dan.

It's hard to see past our own grief. Grief is a selfish bastard.

We never truly mourned as a family. None of us did.

We got on with things, because we knew no other way. I honestly believed that if I stayed strong, and held it all together, then you children would do similarly. We would survive it all, and, in time, we'd adjust.

Not forget. Adjust.

Trev came to work with me. Your sisters took on the role of mother to you, despite them only being children themselves.

We each had duties to fulfill, tasks to perform, a routine to adhere to.

And you were floating around amidst that.

A year passed. And another. You started school, and the pressure dropped somewhat. Repeat, repeat, repeat. Keep going; keep rotating; keep the point in the groove. As soon as it stops, turn it over and begin again. Drown it out with motion and sound.

All of that said, you were a wonderful child.

Thanks for making it easy.

You were always content to simply be. You had an ability to occupy yourself for hours with not much more than your imagination or some pencils.

I'd sit you in my Record Room on a Sunday afternoon, music always playing, and you'd tap your feet together in time to it as you played with whatever held your interest.

You loved art, and would spend hours colouring with your crayons.

When you were five, you drew a picture at school.

"Is that me?" I asked you, pointing at a person you'd depicted.

"Yes, daddy!"

"And what am I doing?"

"Holding a record."

"Why did you draw me holding a record?"

"Because it's what you do."

"And who's that?"

"Mummy," you said sadly, and hung your head.

Take a look. The picture is inside the cover, if you haven't already seen it.

You drew Paula with a purple scarf covering her head. That was your memory of her. It was how you knew her.

"And what's mummy doing?"

"Painting her art!"

"Why?"

"Because that's what she did."

"No, she didn't, Danny. She wasn't an artist."

"She was! She was always painting with her hands. She always smelled of paint."

"No, son."

"Yes! When she was sad, she painted!"

I couldn't understand. Your mother had never been an artist. She'd sketch out designs for Ally Mac with a pencil, but was never very artistic. They were basic crude depictions of what was in her mind. She never painted, as far as I knew.

Were there things I didn't know? Did you know things that I didn't? Did she have secrets, and why wouldn't she have told me?

I looked again at the picture you drew. The red paint was only on her hands.

"Oh, Danny," I said to you, and scooped you up.

"She did paint, daddy. She did," you insisted.

"Yes she did, you clever lad. She painted her fingers, son. She lost her hair, and the chemo discoloured her nails, so she painted them red. Every day, she painted her nails."

"She was an artist, daddy, wasn't she?"

"Yes she was, son. She was a wonderful artist!"

Love, Dad x.'

47.

We sit in a pub back in Tredmouth.

"So, no pressure, but what do you think of the place?" he asks me.

I grin at him. "I think you already know."

"I figured it might suit you, from what you said on the phone."

"How much a month?"

"That depends."

"On?"

"On whether you fancy working for me or not."

"Working for you?"

"Yep. You need a job, don't you?"

I nod. I do. I can't sell dad's records. They're mine now, and I'm keeping them. Any income from Tommy Histon won't be enough.

"I only thought about this when I walked into the house today," Chris says, "and I saw all of the records on the shelves."

"I don't understand."

"I've been thinking about something for ages now. Of course, you'll know better than me, but there's this vinyl revival thing going on."

"Yes, it started around the time my dad died."

"Well, I've got the pressing equipment from back in the day. It's sat there gathering dust for over thirty years, and I'm thinking about resurrecting it."

"Where is it?"

"It's in an old house near Norton Bassett. My father used it as a recording studio, and pressing plant."

"Chemisette Records," I point out.

"You know about that?"

"Yes, through my dad."

He smiles knowingly.

"Of course, of course. Well, then you mentioned your experience at the paper, the articles you're writing, and your chemistry degree, and I thought, this is a bit too good to be true."

"What is?"

"I need a manager. A manager come A&R man, come marketing person, I suppose."

"Me?"

"Why not?"

"Because I don't know anything about pressing..." I pause for thought. "I'd love to do that. But I don't have any experience."

"I know where the expertise is, Dan. It's sitting around waiting for me to give it a green light. But I need someone I trust to pull it all together."

"So, what, relaunch Chemisette Records?"

"Yep. It's something my father would want. And we can offer the pressing service to other labels and bands. Oh, and I'd like to get the recording studio up and running again."

"You could press the Tommy Histon record," I throw in.

"What Tommy Histon record?"

"You've heard of him?"

"Of course! My old man would tell some stories about that. How he and Ally Mac paid for him to come over from America, and funded his recording, and he killed himself after destroying all trace of it."

"Ah."

"What?"

"Was he angry about that, your dad?" I fish.

"Nah. He'd shake his head at it all. He'd just like to tell the story. My old man and his stories. He had a few of them!"

"Good."

"Why?"

"Because I have the only surviving copy of those tracks."

"Kimono For Kip?"

I nod and raise my eyebrows at him.

"You're fucking kidding me?" he asks, but with a smile lighting him up.

"Nope. Tommy left them with my dad, and swore him to secrecy."

Chris throws his head back and guffaws, as he bangs the table with his hands.

"Priceless!" he eventually says, "so, Bill Goods had the goods for all of these years?"

"Yes. You know what I'm thinking?"

"Go on," he says.

"Wouldn't it be apt, if the first release on the new Chemisette Records, was what should have been the first release on the original Chemisette Records?"

"Imagine the publicity!" he exclaims, his eyes wide.

"Exactly."

"But what about the rights. Who owns the rights?"

"I do. Well, my family and I do."

"Do you ever get the feeling something is meant to be?"

"Yes. And I'm probably meant to buy you another drink right now."

"I'll get them."

"No, Chris. If you don't mind, think of it as my dad buying your dad a drink, as an apology for keeping a secret for fifty years."

"In that case, get them in."

I stand to go to the bar.

Before I can leave, Chris holds my arm, "so, you'll come and work with me on this, Dan?"

"I'd love to. When do you want me to start?"

"Tomorrow. Next week. As soon as you can."

"I need another week, if that's okay?"

"Of course. A week on Monday, then."

"A week on Monday."

We shake hands on it, and I go to get two pints from the bar.

A sign thereon reads, 'Bill Of Fare'.

It makes me smile, that sign.

48.

'01211 - Lee Hazlewood - Forty'.

'Hello Danny, my boy.

Do you know, this record was never released in this country? I don't know why not.

This is an American copy that I picked up in a second-hand shop in Oakburn on a Saturday in October of 1983. I have even less of a clue as to how it ended up there.

It must have a story to tell.

My story is, I'd recently turned forty, so the title appealed. That said, I'd have bought it anyway. I paid fifty pence for it, and it had evidently hardly been played.

Sadly, they used non-peelable price stickers, so there is a small scar where I removed it. Use a little bit of washing-up liquid, son. Or just leave it on there. It's all part of the tale each record tells.

Seriously, how did the record come to be there? How did it cross the Atlantic, and end up in a junk shop in Oakburn?

I was there because I couldn't think of anywhere else to be.

Nothing felt real. Paula, Shorty, Aunt Bet and my parents were gone. Everything that had once anchored me had been removed, so I felt adrift. I had a sense that I would float aimlessly, or crash on the rocks.

And I didn't know which option I preferred.

It never once occurred to me to do anything daft. Suicide didn't cross my mind.

It's more accurate to say, I didn't care about the consequences of anything. I didn't want to die. But I didn't really want to live either.

I was depressed, son.

That's clear to me as I think back on it. But depression wasn't recognised and understood in the same way it is now.

Back then, it was seen as weakness. It peppers our language, that approach.

Pull your socks up. Pull yourself together. Stiff upper lip. Chin up. What doesn't kill us makes us stronger. Keep calm and carry on.

So that was what I did.

But I was only half the man that I had been before.

That half was what I presented to the world. That was my outer-self. My inner-self was a scrambled, liquid mess. Nothing worked properly. Every filter was blocked. My plugs held just sufficient charge to get me started in the morning. And as long as I didn't break down, I could just about keep going.

So I went to Oakburn that day, so I might not stop.

You kids were at my sister's, and I had the day to myself. That worried me. That was the worst time. You four gave me momentum.

Nothing interested me.

The only music I wished to hear was the music from the past; the records I shared with Paula. Through them, I could hang on to some tiny part of her.

Even the Lee Hazlewood LP is from a time when I was with her - 1969. Mr Hazlewood had turned forty himself that year. I liked the symmetry of it.

I paid my fifty pence, and felt something as I went to leave the shop. Some muscle-memory was triggered by the simple act of holding a record in a bag in my hand, and walking with it.

It conjured up a time when I strode from a shop in Millby as a cocky fifteen-year-old who bought the right wrong record.

And I saw myself arriving back at my old flat, Tim Hardin's debut in my hand, only to discover that Madeleine Michey was gone.

But she had to go, Dan. She had to leave so Paula could come back in her place.

It led to me seeing myself walk from Ally Mac's home, two records in my possession. And, just as then, I set the record down in the footwell on the passenger side.

Muscle-memory leading to real memories. All of it through vinyl records.

It was so real that I turned my head, expecting to see Ally Mac by my window, ready to ask me about his clothes, and to warn me not to upset my beautiful Aunt Bet.

And there he was! She was, more accurately!

It was unbelievable. Because it wasn't real.

The permed brown hair, blouse and skirt, and bright red lipstick belonged to the woman from the second-hand shop.

She was waving at me, trying to get my attention. So I lowered the window.

"Is everything okay?" I asked.

"Oh, yes, darling. Nothing to worry about. It's regarding the record you bought."

"Oh. Do you need it back?"

"No! It's just, well, we got a load in yesterday. About two hundred, I think. That was one that fell out the box, so I popped it in the case where we have a few books for sale. It's not really our thing, to be honest."

"I don't understand," I admitted, "was I not supposed to buy it?"

"Yes! Yes you were. I just wondered if you'd be interested in seeing the others. It'll save me having to find room for them. As I said, we don't really do records, but they were part of a house-clearance. Anyway, if you fancy having a look, you'd be very welcome."

"I'd love to. Thanks," I beamed at her.

Fifteen minutes later, I was driving back towards Palmerton Chase with a boot weighed down by two hundred and more pristine vinyl records.

In addition, for the first time in months, I had a smile on my face.

Eighty quid the lot, Dan. And there are some beauties in amongst them.

Thus, I was repointed. I had a notion to sell any duplicates, of which there were several, but I never did.

I couldn't let go.

And as I sat in my room playing Lee's 'Forty', I understood that I shouldn't have to.

Moving on didn't mean letting go.

In actuality, Dan, of my sixty-nine years on earth, Paula was only present for less than a quarter of them, when you tot it up.

Yes, she was the most important thing to ever happen to me.

But she was dead.

Through Trevor, Beth, Yvonne and you, my boy, she would always be with me.

And so I grieved that night in my room as I listened to this LP.

Come the following day, I awoke, rose, collected you kids, and we went to the pub over by the canal for Sunday lunch.

We toasted your mum, Danny.

Me with a beer, Trev with a shandy, the girls with lemonade in real glasses.

You with a baby lemonade in your vinyl cup.

Darren finally joined us. Peaches had broken down about a mile away, so he'd walked the last part.

We laughed, the six of us. And we told stories.

And I had no doubt that we would all be fine.

Because death isn't the end. Not when you have memories.

I'll see you later, son.

I love you.

Dad x.'

49.

Twenty-One Months Later

Having woken naturally and risen at seven, I cycled forty kilometers around two cups of tea and some fruit. I worked half a day at the pressing plant, and sent everyone home early to be with their families and friends.

I drove home in my five year old cream Fiat 500. My brother maintains it for me.

It was a very good year.

It's Christmas Eve, and I split the tape on the last box, numbered ninety-eight.

And it feels like Christmas. The slight sadness that, as a child, always accompanied the opening of the final gift is here now, just as it was back then.

For one last time, I savour the smell of the plastic outer-sleeves, as it mingles with the vinyl and rushes up to meet the air in the room.

There were no more letters after 1983.

I've played every record, and searched each sleeve, but there were no further adventures of Bill Goods to be read.

I understand why. That life ended when my mum died.

Also, I know the rest of it. I was present.

Rightly or wrongly, dad presumed I had my own tales worth telling after that point in time.

Either that, or he died before he could finish.

Don't we all.

I did find a few bits of paraphernalia.

'05511 - The Wannadies - Be A Girl'.

Inside was a Father's Day card from 1996. I was sixteen.

It read, 'Dear dad. Happy Father's Day! This is the album with the track on that I was playing, and you said you liked. It's called 'You And Me Song'. Love, Dan.'

'06001 - Clinic - self-titled'.

A post-it note on the inner-sleeve reads, 'Holding for Danny. He left it behind when he moved out to go to university in 1999. Song called 'Evil Bill'. Oh dear!'

The final box is lighter than the others, being only about two-thirds full. There are, perhaps, fifty to sixty LPs in it.

A few more days and I'll be done. The end of the journey shall have been reached.

It'll all be over as a new year dawns.

Occupying the vacant space in the box is my dad's record bag.

He was delighted when he discovered it in an outlet store many years ago.

On one of my rare visits home, he lit up when he showed it to me. He'd measured it in the shop, but wasn't certain of its proportions until he could get home and test it with an actual LP.

"You think a record is twelve inches," he informed me, "but with the jackets and plastic sleeves, you have to allow at least twelve and a half. Ideally, thirteen, because you don't want to cramp them. Same with the shelving. People make that mistake all the time, buying twelve inch high shelving for their records, and it won't work. You'll scuff the edges taking them in and out!"

"Right,' I said, not even attempting to hide the boredom from my voice.

"And you want the shelving segmented, or the records will topple, and you can't look through them properly when the shelves are too long like that."

"Right."

"But this bag is perfect, see? And it's padded on the back and front, with reinforced edges running round the four sides. See what I mean? Bloody perfect, it is. Only a fiver. I should have got a couple, but they only had one on display."

"Right."

"How many albums do you think I could fit in there, Dan?"

"Dunno."

"One way to find out, I suppose. I'll fetch some. I reckon I can get a dozen in, no problem. Fifteen more like, looking at it. What do you think, Danny? As long as they're not doubles in gatefolds. I mean, it's a rare thing for me to buy more than a dozen albums in one go. Bloody perfect, it is!"

"Yeah."

"Here, you hold it open while I put the records in. Dan? Can you hold it a tick?"

"I'm busy, dad."

"Ah, work, is it? Email, or whatever?"

"Yeah," I lied. I was playing a game on my phone.

"Not to worry! You make sure that newspaper gets to print, son. I'll do this.

"You know, it wouldn't surprise me to learn this bag was made for records. From before, you know. Before CDs took over. I suppose it's why it was in the outlet shop. Nobody wants them nowadays. A CD will fit in your pocket. What do you think, Dan?"

"It's for a fucking laptop, dad, for fuck's sake."

I take his bag from the final box and cuddle it to me.

"Sorry, dad. It's perfect," I whisper into the fabric.

50.

'07671 - Madness - Oui Oui Si Si Ja Ja Da Da'.

It's the penultimate record my father ever bought.

I've never heard it or anything from it. But it ties back in to the ska music he was so fond of, thanks to Darren Smith.

There's a lovely track on it about 'Never Knew Your Name'. How was that not a massive hit?

A quick search on the internet reveals it was released just a couple of weeks before dad died in late-2012.

Did he simply buy it because it was Madness? Or did he hear a track on the radio, and get it because he liked what he heard?

Did it make him think of Trevor and Darren, transporting him back to 1980, when I was born, and Trev wore a daft porkpie hat I recall from a photograph of my brother awkwardly holding a newborn me?

Dad was by his side on the sofa. My sisters were perched on the arms.

Mum wasn't in it.

Oh shit. She must have taken it.

It's a good photo, that one. Mum must have picked up some of the expertise from when she was a model.

It's a gatefold sleeve for the double LP, which I empty on both sides and peer through.

There's no letter inside.

When the record's finished, I slip it back into the inner sleeve, A-side facing the front. I rotate it so the open side is protected, before sliding it back into place.

Sides C and D prolong the adventure.

Until, they too, come to an end.

'07672 - Cocoanut Groove - Madeleine Street'.

A faultlessly apt title.

The final record.

This is it.

From 'Songs Our Daddy Taught Us' in 1958, to this fifty-four years on.

Again, I've never heard of it.

Before I play it, I look it up.

I think I do that to delay the moment.

It's a Swedish record from four years before dad died. It's described as 'Independent Rock & Pop'.

I'm glad his final purchase was something reasonably contemporary, rather than something harking back to the past.

How did he hear about it? How did he get it?

Did he simply take a punt, and buy it because of the name Madeleine?

Looking at the sleeve again, there's a young man carrying a guitar and leaping over a puddle. He wears a red and white striped top.

I had a top just like it when I was a teenager. Was that what attracted him to it?

It was difficult for him to leave the house by the end, so visits to record shops or fairs were out of the question.

He must have ordered it from somewhere. Not being one for technology, I can't imagine him scouring the internet looking for things to buy.

How?

Did Trevor help him?

My stomach kicks and my heart rises in my chest as I see something white inside the sleeve.

Drawing it out, my heart sinks as I learn that it's a CDr of the album.

That's happened a few times lately, but it was always a CD or a download voucher.

How strange it is, that the things which were supposed to replace vinyl records are now given away free with them.

There's no letter explaining anything, and I'm left with so many unanswered questions.

All that remains to be done, is to play the record.

This final piece of vinyl he ever got to own. Forty minutes or so, and it'll all be over.

A vinyl resting place, I suppose.

I bet somebody's already thought of that.

Without need of thought, I adeptly slip the vinyl from the inner sleeve, my thumb clamping the edge instinctively. My middle digit sits supporting the record, bent away so my nail can't scratch the vinyl. It rests, perfectly balanced on the pad of my finger.

Am I connected with the exact spot where my dad made contact?

In every sense.

Rotating my right hand, I seamlessly find the edge of the platter, as my left hand locates the opposite side - three o'clock and nine o'clock.

Down it goes, onto the turntable, no adjustment required, the central prong threading the hole. Barely touching the sides.

I handle it with all the love and care that he did. He taught me it all.

A velvet brush is swept around the playing surface, going away from the needle, so any dust and debris is removed, and not jammed into the peaks and troughs that deliver the message and tell the story.

My helping hand sets the belt-driven deck in motion, overcoming the inertia and not stretching the belt that I replaced a few weeks ago, along with the stylus.

The cartridge should be good for a few more months.

I catch the energy my finger introduced, and flip the switch to activate the motor.

Thirty-three and a third revolutions every minute.

I look down on the record, and see my vague reflection looking back up at me.

I smile.

And I spot my father in the image, smiling back up at me.

As I get older, I can see we weren't so different, he and I.

My index finger brings the tonearm over, and without need of the lever that raises and lowers, I lightly deliver the point of it all to the rotating world of music beneath.

It settles with the barest of sound, and is drawn in by the spiral-cut groove.

As soon as it begins, I understand why dad desired this record. It has a sixties feel to it, not unlike The Zombies and The Hollies, I suppose. There's a delicacy and beauty to the songs.

A fragility.

Everything he loved in his music.

Closing my eyes, and leaning my head back on my comfy chair, I attempt to deprive myself of all sense bar hearing.

It's a beautiful listen.

Side one finishes too quickly.

Side two strikes me as being even better. Just as good, at least. No filler here.

I count the tracks, because I know how many there are from the sleeve. Five on each side. I'm counting down to the end of an adventure. A journey of discovery.

The final track on the final side of the final record.

I hope it has a locked groove, so that it might never end.
'Madeleine Street'.
'Seems such a long time ago now.
Took a walk down the street, like a record on repeat.
I can't seem to let it all go.'

51.

It took me ninety minutes to cycle north through the countryside to Norton Bassett.

There was no rush, having allowed two hours, so I savoured the journey.

At the check-in desk, I state my reason for visiting, and point out that I telephoned yesterday. It's the lady I spoke with, and she remembers my call.

I head outside to fill the few minutes I have to wait.

The place is nice. It's the kind of facility I wouldn't mind ending up in.

It's assisted living, but not too assisted. Most of the residents appear perfectly capable of helping themselves, as they stroll the green lawns on this pleasant early-afternoon.

Some wander alone with their smiles and memories, or sit reading a book through thick-lensed spectacles. Others walk in pairs, as, I imagine, new romance or friendship blooms in people who feel younger as a result of it.

Still others sit in groups, either chatting or enjoying a game of some description. Either way, they laugh.

Yes, it's a happy place.

It's a place people come to for company, I sense. It's better than being alone.

One man sits with his legs outstretched, earphones clamped to the sides of his head. His finger taps on the arm of his chair in time to music unheard by me.

I wonder what he's listening to?

He appears to be about dad's age, were he still alive.

I smile and point at him. He slips the phones off one ear and raises his chin at me by way of inviting a question.

"What are you listening to?" I ask.

"Oh, an old album. Of course, it's not old at all. It's a CD. But I had the vinyl back in the day. You're too young to remember proper records, I expect."

"Don't be so sure of that," I reply lightly.

He looks at me dubiously.

"So, what is it?" I ask again.

Rather than answer, he hands me the CD case that was tucked down by his side.

I recognise it immediately.

"Les McCann," I read aloud.

"As I said, before your time."

"It is. But I know it came out in 1966 on the Limelight label in the USA. My father had that version. The UK release was on the parent label, Mercury. It's nice soulful jazz. I didn't realise you could get it on CD."

"My granddaughter picks them up for me. Funny thing is, I remember my wife falling pregnant with our Stuart when this came out. Yes, I suppose it would have been 1966."

"Enjoy it," I say, and leave him to his memories.

He waves a hand and slips the phones back over his ears.

"Are you Daniel?" a female voice asks.

"Danny," I clarify, and turn to see a pretty woman in her mid- to late-thirties, I should think.

She's tall and slim, but still curvy. Her hair is neck length and fluffed out. Her eyebrows tell me she's naturally quite fair, but not as blonde as her hair is coloured.

Her hand meets mine, and I feel a little kick in my stomach at the contact.

I'm fully aware of the fact I find her attractive. Moreover, I believe she experienced a similar sensation.

I'm unsure why I think that.

I smile, close-mouthed, and nod my greeting.

"I'm Rachel," she informs me, and I repeat her name in my head three times so I shan't forget it.

"Nice to meet you, Rachel," I say, further logging her moniker by stating it out-loud.

"Please, follow me," she invites, and I walk a pace behind her. It's impossible for me not to take in her figure as I do.

What is it with health care professionals? Are they all this attractive? I should have switched chemistry for something more medically based.

I follow her into a room, where a woman sits by a large window with her back to us. Two other chairs are situated by a low table.

"This is Helen Clancy. Well, Helen Jarvis now," Rachel introduces us.

I gently take the small brittle hand that I'm offered, and am surprised by the warmth it holds.

"I'm Danny," I inform her, and she smiles, her face craggily erupting and demonstrating her character and life.

She's a pretty woman, despite the age that shows. Her eyes remain sharp, and she made an effort to receive her visitor. There's a hint of lipstick in place, and a brush of blush along her prominent cheekbones.

I'm delighted that Rachel stays in the room with us.

"This is my granddaughter, Rachel," Helen says in her strong and steady voice. It belies her tiny frame, her voice.

And I suddenly see the family resemblance.

"You're younger than I thought you'd be," Helen adds.

"I was the baby of the family. My parents were nearly forty when I came along."

"Any brothers and sisters?" she asks, making smalltalk.

I think she may be a little nervous, meeting me. I didn't tell her what it was about. Just that I was Bill Goods' son, and would it be possible to come and see her.

"One brother, two sisters. Trevor is eleven years older than me. Beth nine, and Yvonne seven."

"And your father, is he well?"

"Ah, no. I should have explained. He died about eight years ago."

"I'm sorry."

Rachel sits quietly next to her grandmother. I sit facing the pair of them.

"Thank you."

"He wasn't very old."

"No, he was sixty-nine when he died. But you probably worked that out." I briefly chuckle at myself. It's nerves.

"Would you like a cup of tea or coffee, Danny?"

"No, thank you."

"He broke my heart, you know?" she says suddenly, but not sadly.

"Yes, he worried about that. That's kind of why I'm here."

"Oh," she says, regarding me with her bright eyes, "did it take you all those years to track me down?"

"No, it was pretty easy, thanks to the internet. But I did think about coming here for a few months."

"Well, you came!"

"I did. He left me his record collection when he died."

"He loved his music, did Bill! Back then, I mean."

"He never stopped," I inform her, "and in certain records he left me notes. Letters, I suppose they are. He left them in the ones that held memories, both good and bad."

"Oh dear. And he left one on me. Was it good or bad?" she asks, and I see a flicker of concern flash across her eyes.

Rachel takes her hand.

"It was in a Ray Charles album that he bought just before Valentine's Day in 1960."

The date resonates with her. A sadness descends like a mesh covering her face. It renders her a little ashen and dull.

I swiftly continue. "He was very upset by what took place. He regretted it his whole life, if that means anything to you. He wrote to me that, whilst there wasn't much in his life he'd go back and alter if he could, what happened between you and him was something he would change."

"Too late now," she points out, reasonably.

I nod.

She adds, "I was all set to go to university. I had all these dreams, Danny. I actually thought that, once I had my degree, Bill and I would marry. And because of what happened, I did something stupid with a boy. And it changed the course of my life. Now, at the time, I was depressed about it. I believed I'd ruined my own life through one bad decision."

I sit and listen. That's my role here for now, to allow her to tell her story. It's what I should have done with dad.

Turning slightly towards Rachel, she takes her granddaughter's hand in both of hers.

"But I was silly. It wasn't the ruin of me - it was the making of me! Because that, Rachel, was how your father, James, came to be, and it's why you're sitting here with me now. I wouldn't alter a thing," she concludes, turning back.

Addressing me, she carries on, "I've had a wonderful happy life, Danny. I won't deny it was difficult being a single mum back in those days. But I met a beautiful man, a kind and loving gentleman named Ken, and he married me in 1962, and took James as his own. We had five more children, you know? Six in total! And I have... Oooh, I lose count sometimes. How many grandchildren is it, Rachel?"

"Seventeen, gran."

"Seventeen grandchildren. And, let me think a tick, nine great-grandkids! I'm the luckiest woman in the world, Danny!"

"And Ken?" I ask.

Rachel answers, "you were chatting to him outside when I came to collect you."

"Ah, the man listening to the music!"

"Another one mad for his music! You couldn't make it up, could you?" Helen adds.

Smiling, I shake my head in wonderment.

"Jazz for Ken, though. Always jazz."

"My dad liked his jazz a bit, back in the sixties."

"Everybody did, love."

As I lean down to retrieve the envelope from my bag, I wonder if I should show her.

But it's why I came. I think dad would want me to.

I hold it, and prepare to explain. I'll let her take it from me, if she desires.

"He kept the Valentine card you gave him that day, Helen. It was inside the Ray Charles record I mentioned, along with the letter to me."

"Oooh, is that it?" she asks, brightening.

"No. This is the one he wrote for you that day. I don't know if I'm doing the right thing. But I thought, probably stupidly, that you should have it."

"What does it say?" she asks, the nervousness back as she settles her hands in her lap.

"I have no idea. It's been sealed for sixty years."

"Oh my!"

"Yes. Look, I can leave now, and take this with me. It's your call," I propose, holding the envelope by its edges, as I would a record.

"What do you want to do, gran?" Rachel asks.

"I'd like a cup of tea," she announces, beaming her smile at me, "see if Ken's ready for one, will you Rachel? Please, love."

She leaves us.

As soon as she has, I realise that Helen got her out of the way deliberately.

"No secrets, Danny. That was the rule I made for myself all those years ago. So, if I'm going to look inside that envelope, I want to do it with my husband of nearly sixty years right by my side. Is that okay?"

"Of course."

"Now, will you have a nice cuppa?"

"I'd love a tea. Thank you, Helen."

She busies herself filling the kettle and prepping the cups.

"Milk and sugar?"

"Just milk, thanks. Can I help?"

"No, no. You're my guest. You sit there. I did hear something, you know? Years back."

"Oh, what's that?"

"I heard, through a mutual acquaintance, that Bill lost his wife young."

"That's right."

I'm aware that Helen is no longer active in the kitchenette area.

I turn to see what's wrong.

She's looking directly at me. A neutral expression settles and levels her face.

"Was that your mum, love?"

I nod.

And for reasons I don't understand, I'm choking on something that I think might be grief.

It stops me answering.

My eyes sting. I can't breathe.

I feel a heat flush my face and neck.

"How old were you?"

All I can do is hold up two fingers to indicate my age.

She's coming to me, her arms folding around my neck.

I sink into her, this stranger to me. This ex of my father's. One of his stories.

And, for the first time since I was a child, I let the tears stream from my eyes.

52.

I never read what dad wrote in the card to Helen. It wasn't my business.

It was enough to observe her as she paused and drew a breath, a breath she held as she broke the seal that had remained intact for six decades.

She studied the front, a little smile tugging at the corners of her lips.

And she opened it up to see what it contained.

A small laugh sprang forth from her, as she tried to catch it in her hand a moment after it left her mouth.

Too late.

She smiled at me, her eyes glistening with either devilment or moisture. I couldn't tell which.

She held it out to me.

I shook my head, and indicated that she should show it to Rachel and Ken.

They each read it, and appeared happy as a result.

Ken placed it on a display shelf, next to a clock that silently ticked away the seconds that add to minutes and hours. Before becoming days, weeks, months and years. A lifetime.

A life that can silently pass unnoticed, if one isn't careful.

That was five months ago.

I didn't go back. It didn't feel right, despite an invitation from Helen and Ken to call again.

It felt like the past. And I was keen to get on with the future.

This is my life now. This is my future.

A phone call yesterday morning brought me out.

"Hey, Danny, it's Vince from the record shop."

"Hello Vince. What's up? Have you got something for me?"

"Indeed I do. The Bert Jansch record you pre-ordered is in the shop."

"Great stuff."

"It gets better."

"Go on," I urged.

"That Clinic record you're after…"

"Free Reign? Have you got me one?"

"Mint. Still sealed."

"How much?"

"Seeing how I knew your dad, how does twenty quid grab you?"

"Done. I'll be over tomorrow."

"See you then, then."

I was planning on riding the bike over to Palmerton Chase anyway, so a call in at Millby isn't much out of my way.

It's a twenty-five mile one-way trip from my cottage with the deviation. It's not so far.

I've done it before. It's fairly flat in the middle of Brakeshire. No real hills to negotiate.

No hurdles.

Even if there were, I'd find a way.

53.

The weather forecast for this October day is dry and partly cloudy. I ponder what the difference is between partly cloudy and mostly sunny, as I pedal steadily.

Dad's record bag is slung over my shoulder. It flaps around a little in the breeze, being empty prior to my reaching the shop.

In the pannier on my bike are a change of clothes and some bathroom essentials.

I'm staying with Trevor tonight. Beth and Yvonne are coming over for dinner. It's nice. I've done it a number of times. We all get together every few weeks, and have some laughs.

I like having a family again.

I say again. It may be for the first time.

Millby is reached in no time. It sits like a spindle-hole at the centre of a record, the rest of the county revolving around it.

I have a brief chat with Vince, as I inspect the records. The shop's busy, thanks to the vinyl revival. Whatever that is.

I'll have a quick flick through the new arrivals. You never know.

I come in a lot. They know me. Just as they knew my dad. I get a discount. Ten to twenty percent on second-hand records. A bit less on the new releases.

They scratch mine, and I scratch theirs. Not the records, though.

Adding a John Renbourn album to my stash, I pay my forty-five - the speed of a record - and hit the road, Jack.

At least, that was the plan.

Someone holds a reissue copy of 'Songs Our Daddy Taught Us' by The Everly Brothers. The first album my dad ever bought.

"Good album," I say without thinking.

"I'll let you know when I've played it."

I look up to see Rachel.

It takes me a second or two to piece it together, that she's Helen's granddaughter.

"Hello again!" I say, probably too enthusiastically.

"Oh! Hello!"

"What are you doing here?" I ask.

"I live just up in Oaklea. This is where I come to get CDs for granddad."

"And records for...?"

"Myself. It sounds better on vinyl. I've got all gran and granddad's old records at my house. There's not really room at the place they're in."

"Why are they there?"

"Because I like them," she answers.

"Sorry?"

"I like records."

"No, erm, I meant why are they in the assisted living place? Your grandparents?"

"Oh, I see! They chose to be. They don't want to be a burden, I think. I told them they could live with me, as I'm on my own, but no."

I nod my understanding. She's on her own.

She adds, "I'd better pay. We're causing a hold up."

I wait outside for her.

"Look, feel free to say no, but do you fancy getting a coffee? "

"Oh, I can't."

"Ah, understood. Sorry, I just..." I trail off.

"No, I don't mean ever. I'd love to. But I promised gran I'd be over by one. She's got a hair appointment in Oakburn at half past. And I've got a couple of new CDs for granddad."

"Well, look, I'm going to be cycling back through Millby tomorrow late-morning. How about then? Only if you want to, of course."

"That sounds great. Yeah," she adds, running it by, and confirming it to herself.

"Say, eleven? Right here by the shop?"

"Works for me."

"I'll see you then."

"See you."

54.

The bag lies flatter against my back as I cycle on, the records holding it close to me.

Twenty minutes on - the time it takes to play one side of an album - and I'm out in the sticks.

A wall draws my eye, the free-standing stone structure that interlocks and supports itself. Behind it sits the house once owned by Ally Mac.

Glimpses of it come to me as the tree branches allow. It plays on my eyes like an old film reel, flickering light and dark.

What a wonderful world!

I'm happy. I'm actually perfectly fucking happy.

Riding along on the crest of a wave.

Everything beautiful is no longer far away.

It's almost a Grandaddy track, from 'Under The Western Freeway'. Dad bought the album back in 1997, before I moved away.

The warm wind bathes me, slight on its own, but strengthened by my movement through the atmosphere.

As I freewheel down the gentle slope past Ally Mac's old place, I wonder if there are any records left inside, tucked away in recesses, or dumped in the old cellar?

It could be a treasure trove in there. Jukeboxes filling whole rooms.

I should knock the door one day, and ask.

Faint heart never won fuck all, after all.

I'm meeting Rachel tomorrow. There was nothing faint-hearted about me there.

Ha! I'll always remember, thirty or forty years from now, precisely which records I bought on the day I asked her out.

Jansch, Clinic, Renbourn. There will be a track contained therein, that I'm yet to discover. And the song will hold the memory, so Rachel and I can play it in years to come, and reminisce about the day we met in a record shop in Millby.

Perhaps we'll have children, and I'll, one day, tell them the story as I play them the song.

They probably won't want to hear it, but I'll make them listen. Because it's important, all of that stuff.

Not so long ago, I would never have asked Rachel out like that. And, I dare say, she would never have even noticed me.

Had I not been in that record shop at that moment!

I was always a worrier. I worried about rejection and missing something.

And I was missing something all the while. I was missing out on my own life.

I felt cursed, because of what happened to mum. Yet, here I am, alive, turned forty, an age she never got to see.

"Thank you, dad!" I call into the air.

I feel free, as I close my eyes and coast down the slope, the wind fresh and beautiful all over and around me.

Cleansing.

I'm proud of myself.

I'm on an unstoppable roll.

Rollin' Danny.

Gene Vincent.

The Fall.

Pride comes before a fall...

'Watch out for pride, Danny. It knows.'

I open my eyes on the world before I reach the corner.

Half a second is all I have.
There's nothing I can do.
I see the panic on the driver's face.
And I hear and know nothing at all.

55.

'00154 - Trashmen - Surfin' Bird'.

He replaces it with a sticker he writes out himself.

'Trashmen (US original) Near Mint - £100' is all the information required.

He's been doing this since the early-eighties.

In all of that time, this is the best lot he's ever picked up.

The right stuff in the right condition. A record dealer's dream.

And the price was right. More than right. The seller didn't know what they had. No interest. They were just old records taking up space.

One person's crap is another's treasure.

He's surprised he got it at the price he did. He was expecting to be outbid.

People get greedy. Still, their loss. His gain. Silly bastards.

This will help to finance his retirement. Not that he'll ever retire. He wouldn't know what to do with himself if he didn't go to work in the shop every day.

He picks up the final record in the pile, and grins lasciviously as he slides it from the protective outer sleeve.

The sticker stating '00100 - The Beatles - Please Please Me' is peeled off and discarded.

Tilting the record to the light, he visually inspects it. There's no time to play them all. Time is money.

He knows it's a rarer stereo first pressing at a glance.

An excitement causes his stomach to gently churn.

Squinting, he checks the credits. 'Dick James'.

His grin broadens.

One final examination, as he holds it at eye level, and looks for any warping or bowling.

As he attempts to slip the record back inside the cover, it catches on something.

Sliding his hand inside, he snags and draws out a piece of paper. The delay annoys him.

He has to give it a quick look, in case it's an autograph, or something else that may increase the value.

It's a letter to someone called Danny.

He drops it into the bin by his side.

He writes out a sticker of his own.

'Please Please Me (STEREO) 1st Pressing - Near Mint - £2000'.

It won't go out in the shop. Too good for that. He'll list this lot on-line. That's where the money is.

Affixing it to the front of the album, he moves on to the next batch of twenty-five to thirty records.

Fucking Chipmunks.

He shakes his head. It doesn't even warrant his time inspecting it.

The 'Chipmunks Sing The Beatles' album they did is the only one worth anything. And even that isn't worth much.

Ah well, some you lose.

The plastic outer is removed, and set aside to be used on a better record.

No heed is paid to the handwritten sticker stating '00155 (play) - TH'.

He walks across his shop floor and drops the album in the fifty pence box.

People will buy any old crap, he thinks to himself.

56.

'00155 - Tommy Histon - Kimono For Kip'.

'Dear Billy.

One day, I hope you'll read this note. At the moment, you can't read. That's because you're two days old!

If you could read at two days old, I wouldn't need to go to work!

I want you to know that I'm so proud to have you as my son.

To tell you the truth, I never thought I'd have children. Further, I wasn't sure I wanted children. I know now that I do. You, along with your mum, are the greatest thing to ever happen to me.

From now on, I'll refer to her by her name - Rachel.

The majority of these LPs belonged to my father. You were named for him - Bill.

One day, they will all be yours, and I hope you'll cherish them as he did. And as I have learnt to. But, if you don't, and you choose to sell them, that's your choice. They shall be yours to do with as you please.

There are over eight thousand of them now, as I've added a few hundred in recent times, and Rachel contributed a couple of hundred jazz LPs that were her grandfather, Ken's.

At one time, though, I almost lost three boxes of them.

I almost lost a lot more besides.

A year and a half ago, I was cycling over to Palmerton Chase to visit my brother and sisters. There's a long downhill stretch of road by a house once owned by a man called Ally Mac. I should say lady, really.

Well, I was hit by a car, the driver messing with his phone, trying to play a song.

That resulted in me being in the hospital for many weeks while I healed. I was unconscious for three days.

A couple of years before, I once told a little lie about being unconscious. Never tell lies, pal. They have a habit of coming back to bite you! Trust me on that.

Well, the following day, a Sunday, I was supposed to have met up with Rachel outside a record shop in Millby. Obviously, I didn't make it.

She did. She waited for me for an hour and a half, worried she may have had the time wrong. She went inside to escape the rain.

Just as she was about to give up and leave, a policeman entered and chatted with Vince, the owner.

My name was mentioned, as they attempted to establish a time-line for me from the previous day.

She told the policeman that she was supposed to meet me. He informed her that I was in Millby General Hospital.

Rachel sat with me for the next two days. When I awoke, she was the first thing I saw.

I became aware of my hand being in hers as my senses returned.

For the rest of my life, I desire to hold her hand, Billy. I never want to let go. Unless it's to hold you.

We fell in love with one another over the weeks I was laid up. And when it came to the time for me to be discharged, I needed to go to a place where I wasn't alone.

My brother and sisters offered, because they're such good, kind people, your aunts and uncle.

But, no. I moved in with Rachel, right here in the Oaklea Estate.

It's where I sit now, writing this in my music room. That's what we call it - The Music Room.

You're asleep by my side, as I listen to a Tommy Histon LP. You'll hear all about him.

Rachel is grabbing a couple of hours well-earned sleep upstairs, so we have to keep the volume low.

This wasn't the first song you heard, though. At the moment of your birth, Tim Hardin's 'How Can We Hang On To A Dream?' was playing on the compilation Rachel and I put together in readiness for your arrival.

So, I was set to come home from hospital, and your Aunt Beth handled the moving of my worldly goods from a house I rented a few miles away.

It was my fault, I concede. I told her that anything in the boxes could be sold. It was supposed to have been old computer games, DVDs and other irrelevant stuff I no longer had any use for.

I forgot about the three boxes of LPs I didn't have shelf space for!

They ended up being purchased by a man from a record shop in Tredmouth, who Beth found on the internet.

As soon as I got to Rachel's, I realised what had happened, and went in to a bit of a panic. They contained the first couple of hundred records my father ever bought.

I was incapacitated, but the following is my understanding of how events unfurled.

"Did you buy three boxes of LPs a couple of days ago?"

"I buy a lot of records. What's it to you?" the shop owner snapped.

"They shouldn't have been sold."

"I bought them fair and square."

"And you'll get your money refunded. But I need those records back."

"Like I said, they're mine now."

"Do you know who I am?"

"I don't care who you are."

"Fair enough. But just so you know, my name's Chris Baxter."

I'm told there was a silence you could taste.

Chris filled it with, "now, seeing how I own this row of shops, one of which you rent from me, I would strongly suggest that it's in your interest to be quite a bit more helpful. So, about those fucking records?"

Chris got all of the albums back. Except one.

It was a very rare LP by Tommy Histon. Because it was disguised in a Chipmunks sleeve, it had been dropped in the fifty pence box. Well, someone had bought it!

Did they ever work out what they had? Did they appreciate it?

Nothing has come up on the internet about it, so who knows?

I once refused twelve thousand pounds for that very copy.

I replaced it in the sequence with this reissue that Chris and I released a couple of years ago.

Do you know, my son? I quite like the idea of that record floating around out there somewhere.

Perhaps, one day, it'll be discovered for what it actually is.

Now, that'll be a story worth hearing!

In addition, a couple of my dad's letters to me went missing.

It doesn't matter. I know the content, and so will tell you the tales one day.

I'll write some more soon, Billy.

I love you.

Dad x.'

Ba-bump, ba-bump, ba-bump :

Afterword.

What will happen to your record collection when you go to your vinyl resting place?

"They'll all go - flogged, charities or skipped. My eldest wants them, but I've explained he doesn't have the room for them, or the patience. I'll save some rare/mega bucks ones as 'gifts'. Plus I may get incinerated with a few that I could never give up. CDs? In the bin or over the hedge. What a bloody waste of a life." Steve H in Nottingham.

"I'm hoping that by the time I am due to hop in, I will have no need of material things. That said, the way things are going, I won't be able to hear them if I live too long, so that might make it easier.

"Mine are going on the pyre along with my hifi and me - hopefully I'll be dead when my wife organises it!

"Seriously though, I like the idea of my surviving family keeping some items and selling the rest for what they are worth, but I suspect that, practically speaking, it will be a dealer, landfill or the rising tides that disposes of it." Sean G in Hampshire.

"They will pass on to my children. My granddaughter already has my Ziggy Stardust album cover framed. I had it done for her 16th birthday, as she loves Bowie. I bought the album in 1975.. Never did I imagine I would be handing it down to my Grandaughter for her 16th. I was overcome. In a very nostalgic way." Donna C in London.

"I just don't know.... probably will be shared with my family, and then the rest sold to pay for my funeral...." Mark W in Scotland.

"My wife and three kids will have a true pain in the ass with it. I think they will sell most of it, unless I do it myself before the time comes." Mika L in Finland.

"I assume it will be split between my wife, daughter and son. Hopefully I will outlive my brother who has a secondhand record shop, so he won't be able to get his hands on them." Brian B in Lancashire.

"Sorry, but I do not want to think about it!" Doen B in Germany.

"It depresses me. Unless l get married before l die, all my belongings will be inherited by my sisters or their descendants, and I'd prefer an alternative idea. I'd like to think that l'd make a Will and give my estate to an animal charity. I think my biggest regret is when l started to collect CDs in 1991. Sometimes l wished l'd stopped record collecting in 1990. Sooner or later, your possessions start possessing you." 'Happy' Craig P in London.

"My wife has first dibs, so I expect that she will extract all of hers that I've annexed, and anything on purple vinyl, then my sons can squabble over the rest. When I say squabble, of course I mean they can both try and persuade the other to take the 'dross' after picking out the odd nugget for themselves." Ray C in Scotland, formerly of Essex.

"My Mom threw away all my Dad's records that were pristine. Some lucky guy picked them up from the curb:. Mine will definitely go to my husband, Jet." Jayne Schizo in New Jersey.

"I do have a 'complete' (at least 'standard' and many 'rarities') Fruits de Mer Records collection. I'd like for it to stay that way! I'm sure Ronnie will look after the precious grooves!" Marc R in Cardiff.

"About 5 years ago, I divided my collection into an archive section (= stuff I will almost certainly not listen to before I die) & the rest. The second step (to sell or dump them) has not really happened - well, I sold some stuff which was really embarrassing or doubles on Discogs. But we are talking here about max 2%. I still have more music than I can ever listen to day & night until my death... But what is logical about collections and collectors???

"Maybe Brexit helps. If I have to move one more time, I will certainly not move this heavy collection, but take the money and run!

"Should have died before I got old!" Till W, a German in the UK. For now.

"I plan on arranging to have it auctioned in aid of medicines sans frontiers or a decent refugee charity." Chris M in West Yorkshire.

"They'll be going to my other half and then he can keep/sell whatever he wants. I'm going to make a list of the rarer ones, so that if he wants to sell any of the ones he doesn't like, he'll be quids in. I'd like to take them with me, but practicalities..." Tony S in Yorkshire.

"I'm leaving mine to my neighbours. Well, I'd hate to think they wouldn't have the pleasure of listening to them after I go!" Peter B in central Scotland.

"I plan for my niece and nephew to inherit a whole load of research that they don't want to do..." Graeme L in Hampshire.

"They'll all go to my daughter, if she'll have them. If not, I suppose she'll put them all up for sale." Greg C in Chicago (the place, not the show).

"As the meme goes, 'my biggest worry is that when I die, my wife sells my records for what I told her I paid for them!'

"In reality, my girls would inherit, and they know the value up to a point. And I hope it would see them right in life.

"As long as they don't go to Oxfam or to the tip. Maybe have my Skids blue buried with me." Pete T in Durham.

"We plan on touring Europe in a camper van, plus the world (not in a van), so I will probably sell them all when I reach 60 ish." Chris M in Leeds.

"The wife says I will!" Chris M in Leeds again.

"No, it's happening, why doesn't anyone believe me?" Chris M in Leeds once more.

"Over the next few years, I will sort out a few hundred that are worth the effort of selling via discogs/ebay and sell them, another thousand or so that are worth the kids selling to some mercenary record dealer when I regularly forget who I am, and the rest will become charity shop embarrassments/landfill when I get shipped off to a home." Keith J, he thinks, in Surrey.

The final word goes to my dad.

Me - "Hey dad, what are you going to do with your records when the time comes?"

Dad - "I've told your sister that you're having them."

Me - "What, even the Dire Straits?"

Dad - "...what do you mean?"

Thanks to all who contributed!

*If you enjoyed this book, I'd recommend '**Across The Humpty Dumpty Field**' as your next read.*

Thank you for taking the time to read this book. It is very much appreciated, and we sincerely hope you enjoyed it.

A **Morning Brake** Publication.
Contact morningbrake@cox.net

Other works by Andy Bracken:

Novels set in Brakeshire:
- Reflections Of Quercus Treen and Meek
- The Book Burner
- Clearing
- Across The Humpty Dumpty Field
- The Decline Of Emory Hill
- Worldly Goods

Other novels:
- What Ven Knew
- Gaps Between The Tracks
- Beneath The Covers

Non-Fiction:
- Nervous Breakdown (The Recorded Legacy Of Eddie Cochran)

Printed in Great Britain
by Amazon